Luke's anger flustered Jill

"I want to apologize for that silly business over William. I know what he said sounded awful, but it wasn't exactly true," she explained.

Luke yawned. "Just why do you feel this urge to unburden yourself? Frankly I'm not interested."

"Luke, please believe—"

"Why do women never know when to shut up!" he exclaimed roughly. "So you'd prefer my kisses to William's?"

He pulled her to him and kissed her. Jill stayed passive, too shocked to react. "Oh, Luke!" she whispered. "Luke...."

When he let her go she was trembling, her heart pounding. She stared at him hopelessly, because it was obvious from his expression that his reaction had been quite different from hers.

Harlequin Premiere Editions

Ex Libris

Harlequin
Premiere
Editions

BELOVED
SURGEON
Sheila Douglas

Harlequin Books

TORONTO • LONDON • LOS ANGELES • AMSTERDAM
SYDNEY • HAMBURG • PARIS • STOCKHOLM • ATHENS • TOKYO

Original hardcover edition published in 1978
by Mills & Boon Limited

ISBN 0-373-82107-7

This Harlequin Premiere Editions volume
published October 1981

Printed in U.S.A.

BELOVED SURGEON

CHAPTER ONE

THE evening rush hour in London was at its peak when Sir James Macaulay finished his ward round at Queen's College Hospital. He came out of the side entrance that lay between the main building and the new private wing, pausing on the top step to say goodbye to his registrar and his house surgeon.

'So you're both off for the weekend?' There was a hint of censure in his voice. 'Surely you had a break very recently?'

'Not for a month, Sir James. Not a long break anyhow.' The registrar, Peter Haddon, was polite but definite. 'We've had a pretty gruelling week, haven't we, Jill?'

Jill Bentley, who hadn't worked for Sir James as long as Peter had done, was still a good deal in awe of the great man. 'Just about average for a busy surgical firm,' she said cautiously, and Sir James rewarded her with a warmly approving smile.

'Thank heaven for someone who doesn't mind hard work! Now when I was your age, Haddon, we had no weekends off at all. Worked six months without a break and proud to do it.'

This was a theme his juniors had heard all too often. From behind their chief's back Peter Haddon pulled a face at Jill. 'Sweated labour,' he muttered, relying on the fact that Sir James was a little hard of hearing.

Unexpectedly the surgeon swung round and glared at his good-looking young registrar. 'What was that, Haddon?'

Peter looked discomfited for a moment and Jill stepped in quickly. 'Mr Young's firm will be covering your patients, Sir James, though if you'd rather I stayed...' Jill was a pretty girl in a quiet way, but when she smiled she was almost beautiful.

Sir James had the reputation of being something of a ladies' man, and it was certainly true that his female house surgeons were never plain. Jill had hair like black silk and clear grey eyes; that he liked her was very plain. The annoyed look vanished, to be replaced by a twinkle.

'Nonsense, nonsense, my dear child. Of course you must have your weekend off. Put some roses back in those pale cheeks, eh?' and he patted her smooth young face. 'Good of you to offer, though.' The hospital clock chimed the half hour and Sir James glanced at his watch. 'I've an appointment at five-thirty. Some sheikh's son they want me to see,' and he rolled off majestically in the direction of the private wing.

'What did he do with his time before the Arab invasion?' Peter asked cynically.

Jill ignored this remark because she was still worrying about the weekend. 'Do you really think he doesn't mind? Our taking time off?'

Peter shrugged, slowing his long stride to match hers. 'Old fool! He just likes to grumble. Does it every time. Means nothing.'

Jill didn't approve of Peter's attitude to the older man. True, Sir James was past his best and delegated more and more of his work to his registrars, but his surgical reputation was awesome, his flair for diagnosis a legend. He could be pompous on occasion and a little silly when there was a pretty girl around, but he was one of the greatest names in British surgery, and Jill at any rate was proud to be working for him.

She said this to Peter, who gave her a pitying look. 'Get with it, girl. The old man's a has-been. He'll be retiring next year. Putting his feet up in the Athenaeum, or whatever stuffy club he belongs to.'

'The Athenaeum. I looked him up in *Who's Who*.'

Peter laughed. 'Basking in reflected glory?'

'No,' Jill said quietly. 'I was thrilled when I got this job, and I wanted to find out all I could about him. I'm not like you, Peter, I don't take all this for granted.' They were passing through the great hall of the hospital now, and she waved a hand towards the marble busts of the famous physicians and surgeons of the past. 'I expect Sir James will be among them one day.'

Peter sketched an irreverent salute to the founder of the hospital, whose portrait hung near the foot of the wide main stairway. 'All right, Jill, you've made your point. Stay young and starry-eyed. I suppose it's part of your charm. Going home for the weekend?'

Jill shook her head.

'Where, then?'

'Nowhere special. I might have a day at the seaside if the weather stays good.'

Something wistful about her manner made Peter give her a thoughtful look. 'At a loose end? Why's that?'

Jill took it as a casual question, made a light reply and departed in the direction of the residents' dining room. She found it nearly empty, took a seat at a corner of the big table, and sipped disconsolately at half-cold tea. It was at times like this that she envied those of her friends who had happy homes and the surety of a warm welcome from loving parents. After an exceptionally busy week she would have welcomed a quiet weekend off in the country. She even toyed with the idea of telephoning her father and saying she wanted to come down. Her father would say yes, of course, but he would be quietly harassed all weekend. As for her stepmother and her half-sister, Betty, between them they had developed to a fine art the technique of making Jill feel unwanted, without actually putting it into words.

That was why Jill had been so excited when she was accepted as a medical student at Queen's College Hospital. It had been a chance to get away from the home that was no longer a true home, after the death of her mother. She could have gone to Bristol University, which was nearer her home in South Devon, but she had chosen London because it was further away, and it represented a fresh start. An exciting, exacting career, a life of her own in new surroundings.

Jill had sailed through her student days, collected a wide circle of friends and achieved a gold medal in medicine. She had been lucky enough to win the coveted post of house surgeon to Sir James after six highly successful months as a house physician. There was absolutely no reason for this absurd fit of the blues, just because none of her special friends were free for the weekend, and she faced two days more or less on her own.

She would go to that concert at the Festival Hall on Sunday evening, she decided, and tomorrow morning she might as well attend the symposium on heart disease at Queen's College. Her last chief, who was one of the organisers, had urged her to go. She stared into her teacup a little forlornly, and looked up with a start when Peter Haddon spoke beside her.

'Why did you dash off like that? I say, you do look downhearted!' He slid into the chair opposite her and tilted it back to an alarming angle. 'What's wrong, Jill? Sometimes it helps to talk.'

Jill liked Peter, though she didn't know him very well. Beneath the offhand manner and the disrespectful attitude to his seniors, there was a kind heart and a sharp brain—she had discovered that much at least in the three weeks she had been on Sir James' firm. Peter had helped her in the operating theatre when she was nervous and unsure of herself, guided her through ward rounds and stood up for her to the Resident

Surgical Officer, that ferocious and uncompromising perfectionist to whom all the junior doctors were answerable.

So she told him a little about her family problems, doing her best to be fair, both to her father and her stepmother. 'After all, it can't have been easy for her, acquiring a four-year-old daughter. I expect it's partly my fault that we don't hit it off. But it's a pity,' she ended sadly. 'I could have done with a break from London.'

Peter brought his chair down with a little bang. 'Then have one. Come home with me.'

When he had convinced her that he really meant it Jill thanked him politely, but said she couldn't possibly accept. 'An extra person out of the blue? A bit hard on your parents!'

'My grandparents, actually. And they love visitors, especially young people. It's settled, then—you're coming.'

'But...' she weakened. 'Where do they live, Peter?'

'In Sussex. Off the beaten track. Just what you need.'

'It would be nice,' she admitted, 'but shouldn't you telephone them first?'

'I'll telephone them later, but I know it'll be all right,' he said easily, and Jill felt a momentary pang that she couldn't invite friends to her home with such assurance. Peter had a date that night. He was taking one of the staff nurses to the latest hit musical, so he wouldn't be leaving until morning. 'Around ten,' he suggested, 'I plan to make a night of it.' He grinned and left her, and Jill, who knew that he couldn't have had more than two hours' sleep last night, marvelled at his energy. With the prospect of an enjoyable week-end ahead of her she was quite content to potter in her room that evening, washing her long dark hair, packing a few clothes and sinking into bed at the deliciously early hour of nine o'clock.

She slept for twelve hours and the kind-hearted maid on the top floor of the residents' quarters left her to it. When she finally got up it was to a sparkling October day, with a nip in the air that made her shut her bedroom window quickly. Jill loved her room on the sixth floor. It looked out over an interesting vista of chimney pots to the trees of Regent's Park in the distance. She dressed and finished her packing, then went down to breakfast.

There were always a few people who weren't busy, having a late meal. The maids were tolerant because they knew the long hours young doctors had to work. Jill helped herself to toast and coffee, and sat down by Gwyneth Hughes, a lively Welsh girl who was one of her best friends. Gwyneth took in Jill's chunky sweater and neat dark trousers and said she wished she looked as good in pants.

'Where are you off to? I thought you were going to that medical do.'

'I've changed my mind. At least, Peter's changed it for me. He's invited me to go home with him.' Jill looked around. 'Hasn't he come down yet?'

'Peter? Peter *Haddon*?' Gwyneth looked impressed. 'You are going up in the world!'

Jill stared. 'What's so special about Peter?'

'His connections are rather special, wouldn't you say?' and when Jill went on staring Gwyneth began to laugh. 'Well, for heaven's sake, you do know who his grandfather is?'

'Should I?' Jill asked a little helplessly, and Gwyneth laughed again.

'You are funny, Jill. His grandfather is *the* Haddon—Professor Haddon, last but one Dean of this medical school, and just about the most famous surgeon even Q.C.H. ever produced.'

'Yes, all right, I have heard of him,' Jill said crossly, not liking to be patronised even by a good friend like

Gwyneth. 'I just never connected his name with Peter's. He's never mentioned it.'

'Why should he? Everyone knows. Everyone but you!' Gwyneth's sharp, clever face was frankly envious. 'What it is to be pretty! I worked on that firm for six months and Peter never asked me home.'

'He only asked me because I was at a loose end. He's kind really.'

'And a bit of a wolf.' Gwyneth gave her friend a worried look. 'Don't get involved with Peter. He's a fast worker where women are concerned.'

They were sitting on their own, but even so Jill looked round anxiously. She hated hospital gossip and took care not to indulge in it, which was presumably why she hadn't cottoned on to Peter's illustrious connections. She wished now that she had been firmer in her refusal, and not allowed Peter to talk her into going. The peaceful country weekend might become something of an ordeal, for she wasn't used to moving in such exalted academic circles. One thing at least was explained; Peter's casual attitude to the great men of the medical world.

'I wish I wasn't going,' she said under her breath. 'Do you think it's too late to back out?'

'Of course it is. You are an idiot, Jill, you'll probably have a super time. What are you worrying about?'

'I shall feel out of place.'

'Why should you? Your background is O.K., unlike mine.'

Gwyneth had a bit of a chip on her shoulder, because her family were not professional people. 'Now *you're* being an idiot,' Jill retorted, but before she could say anything more Peter turned up. His handsome face had a faintly dissipated look, and he shuddered when Gwyneth asked him if he wasn't eating anything.

'Just coffee. Hallo, Jill. You look quite revoltingly fresh and wholesome in that white sweater.'

'She is fresh and wholesome, so mind you don't corrupt her.' Gwyneth made this remark jokingly, but the smile with which she accompanied it was a little sharp.

Peter, who made no secret of his dislike for bright aggressive females, said coolly that a weekend with his grandparents would be the reverse of corrupting. 'Not that it's any concern of yours.'

As they crawled out of London in the Saturday morning exodus to the country, he enlarged on why he looked on his grandparents' place as home. 'They practically reared us, my brother Luke and me. My father works for the World Health Organisation in all sorts of outlandish places. He couldn't have had us along when we were kids even if he'd wanted to.'

'Your mother?'

'An entomologist, even more dedicated than my father. Apart from their producing us we haven't impinged much on their lives.' His grin dispelled any notion of a deprived childhood.

To Jill it sounded a very odd set-up. 'If I had a family they'd come first,' she declared, 'I'd pick my work to fit in with their needs.'

'Of course you would, because you're a different sort of woman. It takes all sorts,' Peter ended vaguely, and put his foot down on the accelerator as they left the last of the suburbs behind.

'I had no idea your grandfather was Professor Haddon,' Jill said a few miles further on. With faint surprise Peter murmured that he'd thought it was common knowledge.

'Is he ∴ very high-powered?'

'I suppose he was once. Now he's just an old man with a passion for music and chess and gardening. He still reads the medical journals too.' Peter took one hand from the wheel and patted her knee. 'I believe you're nervous about meeting him. You needn't be.'

He added with a little grimace, 'It's my brother Luke who can be the difficult one.'

'Why?' Jill wanted to know, but he only laughed and said she'd find out soon enough.

Just before midday they turned off the A21 and drove through the village of Medhurst. 'Stockbroker country.' Peter waved a hand at the large houses and beautifully kept gardens.

'Or private practice country,' Jill suggested, and he smiled his agreement.

'My grandfather's place is a couple of miles outside the village.'

Jill was prepared for something a good deal grander than her own home, but not for the reality. They turned off the road between massive pillars surmounted by stone eagles, swept round the curves of a long drive, wooded on one side and flanked by farmland on the other, swung round a final bend and on to the forecourt of an old country house. She had a general impression of an elegant façade enhanced by magnificent trees, of wide lawns and well-clipped hedges, then Peter was opening her door and leading her towards the house.

The front door stood wide. They entered a spacious hall and a woman's voice called from a room on the right. 'In here, darling. You're later than we expected.'

'Traffic snarl-up,' Peter explained as he piloted Jill into the drawing-room, where his grandparents sat by a blazing log fire. They rose politely and Peter made the introductions.

'This is Jill Bentley, Grandma.'

She was silver-haired and petite with a charming smile, but a faint air of surprise, quickly hidden.

'And my grandfather.'

Professor Haddon was a gaunt giant of a man with bushy white eyebrows and fierce dark eyes. He stared

at Jill with the same disconcerting expression that his
wife had worn.

Jill swung round to the old lady. 'I've an awful feeling you didn't expect me. Peter promised to ring . . .'

'No, no, my dear,' Mrs Haddon assured her, 'Peter
did telephone. We knew you were coming, and you're
most welcome.'

'But not quite what we expected.' Professor Haddon
clapped a hand on his grandson's shoulder. 'You told
Birdie you were bringing your house surgeon, and she
assumed it was a man.'

'No reason why she should,' Peter retorted airily,
and for Jill's benefit, 'Birdie's our housekeeper.'

Mrs Haddon smiled and patted the girl's arm. 'You
poor child, what a welcome! Peter will show you your
room and then we'll all have a drink.'

She had the easy manner of the experienced hostess,
with the added bonus of genuine warmth and friendliness. Soothed by sherry and Mrs Haddon's gentle
conversation, Jill relaxed and began to feel more at
ease. Peter talked to his grandfather and she caught
snatches of their conversation.

'Luke out?'

'Walking the dogs.'

'Be nice to see him again. It must be over a year.'

Mrs Haddon, catching this last remark, asked Jill if
she had met Peter's brother. 'He was at Q.C.H. until
two years ago—a registrar on the surgical unit.'

Jill shook her head. 'I don't think so. I was never
attached to the surgical unit when I was a student.
Where has he been since then?'

'In the States on an exchange scheme. Luke won the
Dewey-Millar scholarship.' The old lady said this casually, as if it was only to be expected from a member of
the Haddon family.

The Dewey-Millar was the most fiercely contested
surgical prize at Q.C.H., and winning it was a certain

guarantee of future success. Luke must be good, Jill thought. Very good.

'You must be proud of him,' she said politely. 'Is he like Peter?'

A flicker of amusement crossed Mrs Haddon's face. 'Not in the least, my dear. I think that's him now, so you can judge for yourself.'

A door banged, dogs barked, a man's voice shouted at them to be quiet. Then Peter sprang up and rushed into the hall. 'Luke, you old devil, it's grand to have you back. Where did you get that magnificent tan?'

'California,' Luke Haddon said briefly, coming into the drawing-room behind his brother.

Jill's first impression of him was that he was a younger version of his grandfather; tall, lean, strong-featured. A year or two older than Peter, who was twenty-seven. He wore jeans and a thick dark sweater, and in his hands he swung a couple of dog leads. His eyes went to Jill, so Peter introduced them. A little shyly she held out her hand and Luke took it in a strong grip.

'So you're Peter's H.S.!' His deep voice had an undercurrent of sardonic amusement.

'We've been through all that,' Peter chipped in quickly, giving Luke a brotherly thump on the shoulder. 'House surgeons come in all shapes and sizes these days. And a good thing too!'

'Oh, undoubtedly,' drawled Luke, the dark eyes that were so like his grandfather's taking in Jill's mounting and rather becoming blush.

He made her feel horribly shy. Mrs Haddon had been right to say that he wasn't in the least like his brother. Peter was easy to know, charming and out-going, but Luke seemed aloof, sardonic, withdrawn. He said little at lunch, but he had no need to, for Peter monopolised the conversation as he was wont to do in the residents' quarters, telling lively and amusing stories about hospital life.

His grandmother smiled frequently and the Professor gave the odd rumble of laughter. 'Sir James hasn't changed,' he commented, but Luke looked contemptuous.

'I should say he has, and for the worse.' His eyes met Jill's. 'You enjoy working for him, Miss Bentley?'

'Yes, I do!' Jill exclaimed with an unconscious touch of defiance. Did no one in the Haddon family admire her chief?

'Of course she likes working for him,' Peter enlarged, his face split by a huge grin. 'She can twist him round her little finger. When we want something out of the old man we get Jill to ask for it.'

'That's what I meant,' Luke said unkindly. 'It's sad to see a great surgeon degenerate into a silly old man.'

Mrs Haddon stepped in quickly as if she felt the conversation was getting out of hand. 'Really, Luke, that remark was quite uncalled-for.'

Luke accepted his grandmother's rebuke without argument. 'Sorry, Miss Bentley, did I offend you? Nothing personal, I assure you.'

He didn't sound in the least sorry, and that was the moment that Jill started to dislike Luke Haddon. Peter, who wasn't quick to sense undercurrents, carried on with his theme.

'The old boy didn't pick Jill as his H.S. just because she's pretty. The girl's very good at her job ... and very ambitious.'

'Is that so?' Luke asked softly, and studied Jill through narrowed eyes.

For some reason Jill wanted to qualify Peter's statement, to say that she had worked hard as a student as an antidote to her family problems. That no one had been more surprised than herself when she won that gold medal. That she wasn't in the least ambitious.

She would be perfectly content to end up as a small-town G.P. like her father.

Of course she said none of these things. She concentrated on her excellent lunch and did her best to avoid looking at Luke, which wasn't easy as she was sitting directly opposite him. She was relieved when the meal finally ended and Peter announced that he was taking her off to the seaside.

'It's not far to Eastbourne. A walk on Beachy Head will do us both good.'

'Don't be late getting back,' his grandfather requested. 'We've people coming in for drinks this evening,' and she mentioned a few names.

'You forgot the Hendersons,' Luke added. He turned to his brother. 'Shirley's home for the weekend, and looking forward to seeing you.'

There was a tense little silence. Peter stiffened, then said with an obvious attempt at casualness, 'I saw her quite recently. If you don't mind, Grandma, we'll skip the visitors. I was thinking of taking Jill into Brighton for the evening.'

'I'd rather you didn't,' his grandmother said, with the air of one who was seldom disobeyed. She was a gentle autocrat, Jill thought with amusement, deferred to even by the objectionable Luke.

'Well, what do you think of my grandparents?' Peter asked as they raced towards the coast in his red two-seater.

The hood was down and Jill's black hair whipped round her cheeks. Exhilarated by fresh air and speed, she forgot that she had found lunch rather an ordeal. 'They're nice,' she said gaily, 'especially your grandmother.'

'And Luke?'

She wasn't intimate enough with Peter to criticise his brother, so she chose her words carefully. 'Your brother Luke is not an easy man to get to know. I haven't decided what I think about him.'

This flagrantly untrue remark didn't deceive Peter, who gave her a quizzical smile and commented that first impressions weren't always correct. 'I know he's a bit overpowering. They say he's the spitting image of Grandpa as a young man.'

Overbearing would have been an apter word in Jill's opinion. 'Your grandfather was an outstandingly brilliant surgeon,' she said.

'So is Luke,' Peter said simply, and Jill left it at that.

With any luck she wouldn't be seeing much of Luke except at meals, though it was ridiculous to allow someone she had only just met to get under her skin in this way. Thank goodness for a break with Peter! She tossed her hair back, slipped lower in the seat and gave herself up to the thrill of fast driving. They walked for miles along the cliffs, had tea at a hotel and returned reluctantly to the car.

'Grandma's word is law,' Peter said with a grin, 'but it's a pity we can't have a night out in Brighton.'

He was a gay and undemanding companion, and Jill wondered if hospital gossip hadn't rather exaggerated his reputation over women. There had been plenty of opportunity for a little light lovemaking if he had felt so inclined, or perhaps she simply didn't attract him in that way. A modest girl, Jill was inclined to underrate her appeal to men.

They arrived back at only a little after six, but already there were half a dozen cars parked before the house—smart expensive cars most of them, so the Haddons' friends must be well-to-do. Jill was thankful that she had packed a long skirt and a pretty blouse; Peter hadn't been much help on Friday when she had asked him what she should wear.

'Just casual things. We don't dress up in the country.'

A typical man's remark, she thought as she circulated half an hour later with Peter by her side. The women's clothes might be simple, but it was an expensive simplicity, understated and elegant. The long green and gold drawing-room was softly lit by wall lights and standard lamps, the fire had been built up with huge logs, and the heavy floor-length curtains were drawn across the windows. The atmosphere was one of cosy familiarity, for the visitors created the impression of knowing their hosts and each other very well.

They greeted Jill with friendly interest, telling her it was nice to see a new face. How surprising that she was a doctor! And she looked far too young to be qualified! This last remark was made by a poker-backed old gentleman who had just been introduced to her as General Singleton. He went on to say that he had known Peter since he was a child, Luke too, and launched into an account of their boyhood escapades. The General was inclined to go on, but rather a dear. He treated Jill like a favourite niece and she responded in kind.

She was smiling up at him, and listening with genuine interest to a wartime story, when Luke joined them. 'Another drink, sir?'

The General had been patting Jill's arm to emphasise a point, and absentmindedly he went on patting, under Luke's ironic gaze. Colouring, she pulled her arm away. 'I'd like another drink too.' With unusual gaucherie she swallowed half a glass at one gulp, pushed it at him and was relieved when he strolled off towards the drinks table.

'Funny chap, Luke,' the General commented. 'Frightfully brainy of course, but young Peter's more my type.'

This was so exactly Jill's own opinion that she gave the old man a dazzling smile, to which he responded with heavy-handed gallantry. Luke returned at the tail end of this and stood listening, his dark face expressionless, but thinking plenty, Jill was very sure. He showed no signs of going, so after a minute or two, and looking decidedly put out, General Singleton moved off.

'You've made his day,' Luke observed. 'Is that how you handle Sir James?'

She looked at him over the rim of her glass. Careful, she told herself. Keep it cool. Don't let him see how he riles you.

'I like older people. I've always got on well with them.'

'My grandfather's a little harder to charm,' he said drily.

Quick colour flared in her cheeks and her hand clenched round the stem of her glass. Luke noticed at once. 'Look out or you'll break it.' He took the glass out of her hand before she realised what he was about. 'Did I say something to upset you?' he inquired, and she shook her head dumbly, her colour still high.

Perhaps she was too touchy, reading meanings into the man's words that weren't there. It could have been the sort of casual remark that people made at gatherings like this, but Jill had the feeling that Luke wasn't much given to small talk.

'May I have my glass back, please?' she asked with careful politeness, and with a faint smile he returned it.

'I did upset you. I wonder why?' He looked down at her, eyebrows raised, the corners of his mouth tilting upwards in the remains of that maddening smile.

'I'm sure you know why, Mr Haddon.' She must *not* lose her temper. 'Why should I want to charm your grandfather?'

'Only you know the answer to that, Miss Bentley,' he replied with mock gravity, and added under his breath, 'Ambitious was the word Peter used, wasn't it?'

Jill took a deep breath while she tried to think of

some remark that would put him in his place without being too offensive, for she was after all a guest in his grandfather's house. The silence stretched out. Luke wouldn't be an easy man to score off. She glanced around with a well simulated air of interest.

'Who's that girl in the corner? Peter didn't introduce me.'

'Shirley Henderson. Come and meet her. Come on.' When she hung back for a moment he slid a hand under her elbow and steered her across the wide room. Surely Shirley was the name to which Peter had reacted so strongly at lunchtime?

The girl was about Jill's own age, not exactly pretty but fresh and appealing. Luke seemed to like her, for his voice softened when he spoke to her, and Shirley appeared completely at ease with him, in a way that Jill could never be. This was natural enough, seeing that they had grown up together, as Luke explained. He went on to mention that Jill was a doctor and Shirley looked impressed.

'Have you joined one of the local practices?' she asked.

Jill shook her head. 'No, I work in London. The same hospital as Peter.'

'Oh.' Shirley digested this remark, while across her face there flashed a strained look, quickly suppressed. 'You're a friend of Peter's?' The well-bred mask was back in place, but Jill sensed that the other girl waited tensely for her answer.

'Not really a friend,' she said quickly. 'I mean, I've only known him a few weeks. He's my registrar, and —and he only asked me down because I had nowhere else to go. It was very kind of him,' she ended rather breathlessly, because Luke's steady stare had an unnerving effect on her.

Shirley looked relieved and doubtful in about equal proportions. She gazed across the room at Peter, busily engaged in charming a stout middle-aged matron. 'I know. He can be kind—sometimes,' she added bleakly.

The conversation seemed to have run down. Shirley went on watching Peter, Jill could think of absolutely nothing to say, and Luke just stood there, dark and disconcerting, and completely at ease. The matronly woman moved away from Peter and he glanced in their direction. Luke beckoned and his brother came slowly across the room.

'I was thinking, Peter, why doesn't Shirley have lunch with us tomorrow? Be like old times again, wouldn't it?'

Shirley's face lit up and then changed to uncertainty. She seemed to be holding her breath, waiting for Peter's reaction.

'Oh, sure,' that young man said without much enthusiasm. This was one of the times when he wasn't being kind, but perhaps Shirley's wistful adoration was a bit hard to take.

The party had started to break up now and Shirley went off with her parents. 'What did you do that for?' Peter muttered under his breath, as the Henderson family disappeared through the door.

'Why not?' asked Luke. 'She's a nice kid. You could have looked more enthusiastic.'

'Oh, shut up, Luke! I'm beginning to wish you'd stayed in the States.'

At this piece of brotherly rudeness Luke merely laughed and walked off to talk to his grandmother, and Peter said glumly that he didn't see why his week-end should be ruined by Shirley's childhood hangups. Jill was of the opinion, which she kept to herself, that *her* weekend was going to be ruined by her reaction to Luke Haddon.

In bed that night she spent a few minutes brooding on why these strange mutual antipathies sprang up between people, for she was quite sure that Luke returned her feelings with interest. He seemed to think that she was cultivating a friendship with Peter for what she could get out of it. Knowing the right people helped, and there were quite a few of her colleagues who would have jumped at the chance. Only Jill wasn't one of them; she despised the in-fighting and place-seeking that went on among some young doctors. It was unfair of Luke to have labelled her a social climber on such slender evidence. The beastly man had a nasty suspicious mind, so thank goodness that she was un-likely to come into contact with him in the future, and on this comforting thought she drifted off to sleep.

However, at lunchtime next day she was discon-certed to find that she might well be seeing a good deal of Luke in the very near future. The talk had turned to how long a holiday he planned to take after his two-year stint in America.

'Not long,' Luke said briefly, and his grandmother sighed.

'You need a proper holiday after working so hard.'

Professor Haddon dismissed this idea briskly. 'Rub-bish, my dear. Hasn't he just had two weeks in Cali-fornia before coming home?' He bent the ferocious glare on Peter that Jill found so alarming. 'Are there any locums coming up at Queen's?'

'As a matter of fact the R.S.O.'s due for study leave at the beginning of November. We're counting the days, aren't we, Jill?'

The Resident Surgical Officer wasn't popular with the other residents, but Luke would scarcely be an improvement! Jill pointed out that they must have someone lined up to replace him. The job was too important to fill at the last moment.

'I'm not sure they have,' Peter demurred. 'The chap who was originally booked for it has just got a con-sultant's post somewhere else, so he's backed out.'

'There you are then, Luke,' the Professor announced. 'Ring up tomorrow and tell them you're available.'

Luke looked irritated, as if he didn't take kindly to all this family interference. 'I'll think about it,' he said quietly, met Jill's eyes and began to smile. 'Don't you fancy me as R.S.O., Miss Bentley?'

She coloured and tried to think of a light reply. Mrs Haddon came to her rescue. 'Really, Luke, what an odd thing to say!'

Luke's smile broadened. 'Not so odd, Grandma. Miss Bentley has a very expressive face.'

The old lady frowned at him repressively. 'America hasn't improved your manners, my boy.' So might she have spoken to the young Luke.

Shirley Henderson, who had been listening to these exchanges wide-eyed, gave a sudden giggle. 'Oh, I'm sorry, Mrs Haddon,' she excused herself hastily, and Peter stepped in, turning the awkward moment into a joke.

'Of course the poor girl doesn't want two Haddons ordering her around. One's bad enough, isn't it, Jill?'

'For once I agree with you, young man,' his grandmother said caustically. 'Shirley? Jill? Shall we leave them to it? They've been longing to talk shop ever since they sat down.'

As she shepherded the girls into the drawing-room she told them that she drew the line at medicine with meals. It was the one subject she banned. 'Not out of delicacy, my dears, but because they need to get away from it sometimes.'

Jill thought of the enclosed, intense world of hospital life, and nodded her head vigorously. 'You're so right, Mrs Haddon. Perhaps they should make *you* R.S.O.!'

Shirley gave her infectious giggle and while Mrs Haddon disappeared to order coffee, she pressed Jill for more details about her work. When they had met again before lunch she treated Jill rather wearily, but during the meal she had seemed to relax, as if reassured by the casual friendliness with which Peter treated his young house surgeon. Jill guessed that the other girl was really interested in Peter's doings, so she enlarged quite sincerely on what a promising surgeon he was, how popular with the patients, how well liked by the nurses.

'Oh, the nurses!' Shirley looked unhappy at that. 'I suppose he has hordes of girl-friends?'

'I don't think he has time for hordes,' Jill said carefully, trying hard not to laugh. 'I know all those TV serials go on about hospital romances, but honestly, Shirley, our work does come first.'

Later that afternoon the Haddon brothers took Jill and Shirley for a tramp through the lonely woods that stretched for miles behind the house. There were broad rides through the woods, and enticing side paths which led into isolated clearings. Jill, who loved walking, ploughed happily on through fallen leaves, delighted to be out in the crisp October air, and not paying too much attention to the others. She was playing a game with one of the labradors, throwing sticks for him to retrieve, chasing him round and round a thicket, when Luke called from the edge of the clearing.

'Come on, Jill! The others are way ahead.'

Out of breath, she flung herself down on a fallen tree trunk, while the dog subsided at her feet. She felt hot and dishevelled, and remarkably happy, and in her present mood even Luke rated a smile. He crossed the clearing to her, but his answering smile was slow in coming, as if reluctantly given. 'You look about sixteen.' He bent and plucked a twig from her hair. 'Your patients wouldn't believe it if they could see you now!'

Jill stared up at him, conscious for the first time that

most women must find Luke attractive. Peter might have the more conventional good looks, but his brother's impact was quite different. He was tough both in body and in mind, and that was a combination many women admired, except for the few like Jill who resented his air of almost aggressive masculinity.

A scattering of oak leaves blew past them, and a blackbird gave its evening call. 'Come on,' Luke repeated, 'or we won't be home before dark.'

Jill jumped up, brushing her hair back from her face. 'Is it that late? Peter hopes to leave by seven.'

'Wants you to himself for a few hours, I suppose.'

It was more a statement than a question, and it annoyed Jill, because he was jumping to conclusions that simply weren't true. 'Then you suppose wrong,' she snapped. 'He wants to see the new admissions before tomorrow's operating list. And so do I, for that matter.'

She might have known he wouldn't believe her. 'Business and pleasure combined, then,' he commented mockingly, as they set off after the others with the labrador pacing sedately between them.

Jill flashed him a look of pure dislike. 'It's not that way at all. Peter and I aren't interested in each other.'

'He asked you down here,' Luke pointed out, and she swung her arms vigorously to relieve her irritation.

'I told you before—only out of kindness.'

'If you say so, my dear Jill.' He raised his eyebrows at her in the maddening way he had. 'Though a clever girl like you shouldn't have much trouble in getting him interested.'

There it was again, the implication that she was on the make. Luke's view of human nature was cynical to say the least. She stifled an angry reply, because she knew that the spark between them could quickly be fanned into a blaze. There was something more than mere antipathy between them. She recognised that now, though she couldn't have put a name to it. They climbed a steep and muddy path in silence, reached the edge of the woods and saw Shirley and Peter below them, at the bottom of the field.

'Hey, wait for us!' Jill called, and started to run, stumbling in her haste over the rough ground. Hurrying to get away from Luke and the disquieting effect he had on her; relieved that in a couple of hours she would be heading back for London and familiar surroundings.

CHAPTER TWO

Sir James Macaulay's team was first on call from Monday. This meant that in addition to their routine work they accepted all surgical emergencies. There were two registrars and two house surgeons, but even so they would work on average an eighty-hour week.

'There must be easier ways of earning a living,' Peter sighed, as he sat over a midnight cup of tea in Theatre Sister's office, adding a few words to Jill's operation notes. 'What made you go into this racket, Jan?'

Janet Wyman was the youngest of the Theatre Sisters and the nicest. She smiled a little ruefully as she removed her green headscarf. 'If you really want to know, I had ambitions to be a doctor myself. But I didn't make the grade, so this was the next best thing.'

Jan was clever and efficient, so Jill was surprised that she hadn't been selected for medical school. The surprise must have shown, for Jan gave her a very nice smile and said lightly, 'We can't all be lucky. It hurt at the time, but this is worthwhile too.'

A junior nurse poked her head round the door apologetically. 'Sister, we've a problem.' Jan sighed, but went off amiably enough. Peter finished his notes and stretched out his long legs, still encased in rubber boots.

'I haven't had a chance to tell you yet,' he said. 'My brother Luke is going to do that locum for the R.S.O.'

This wasn't welcome news. Jill stared at him, feeling that some reply was called for. 'Who told you?' she managed.

'My grandfather. I rang this evening. And Jill, you've made quite a hit with the old man.' He sounded surprised, as Jill was herself.

Last night when they had left, Peter's grandparents had walked out to the car with them. 'You must come again, my dear.' Mrs Haddon had sounded as if she meant it, and indeed her behaviour all weekend had borne out Peter's remark that she liked young people. The Professor, that man of few words, had given her one of his most ferocious looks, encased her small hand in a bone-cracking grip and rumbled out a 'Harrumph' that could have meant anything. Luke, who had stopped at the front door, had smiled to himself at his grandmother's remark, and gone in again before Peter had even started the car.

'If your grandfather quite liked me your brother certainly didn't,' Jill said wryly.

Peter dismissed her remark with a touch of impatience. 'How can he dislike you? He hardly knows you.'

'Yes, but——' Jill paused a little helplessly, wondering if she might be losing her sense of proportion where Luke was concerned. 'Anyway, I shall do my best to keep out of his way.'

'Jill dear, why have you got such a thing about Luke? He'll be far too busy as R.S.O. to notice your existence.'

Jill wasn't convinced, for the present R.S.O., however hard-worked, could always spare time to criticise his juniors' behaviour. Peter, though, was obviously tired of the subject, and was about to retire to the surgeons' room to change out of his theatre clothes.

Janet Wyman, who had just come in again, stopped him at the door. 'What was that about your brother being R.S.O., Mr. Haddon?'

Peter told her briefly, gave a huge yawn and disappeared. Jan, her usually pale cheeks tinged with colour, sat down and absentmindedly poured herself another cup of over-stewed tea.

'Sister Wyman, that's your fourth cup!' Jill exclaimed.

Jan sipped and pulled a face. 'Ugh! Well, what do
you know! Luke Haddon's coming back!'

'You knew him when he was here before?'

'Oh yes,' Jan said, and let out a long breath. 'I knew
him quite well. Not socially, you understand, but I
was a staff nurse on Lister Ward when he was a
registrar.'

Something about the other girl's manner, and air of
suppressed excitement behind the surface composure,
made Jill pick her words carefully. 'Was he popular? I
found him a little ... spiky.'

Jan smiled. 'You've described him exactly. No, I
wouldn't say he was popular, but he was ... well ...
respected. Everyone knew he was *the* up-and-coming
young surgeon. It'll be ... nice ... working for him
again.'

Jill thought that 'nice' was a typical piece of British
understatement. Sister Wyman was doing her best not
to show it, but Luke's return as R.S.O. had tilted her off
balance to a quite remarkable degree. Jill had only
known her for a few weeks, but she liked and admired
the older girl. As efficient as the other Theatre Sisters,
she was kinder to the junior nurses and far more
tolerant of inexperienced house surgeons. Jan, who
had just changed out of theatre garb, buckled her
Sister's belt about a trim waist.

'Why don't you drop the Sister bit?' she remarked.
'Even Sir James calls me by my first name.'

The girls smiled at each other and parted on the
best of terms. As Jill made her way to the surgical
wards for a last look at the latest admissions, she
thought with pleasure that she had made a new friend.

Their week on take for surgical emergencies was even
more hectic than the last one, but then Jill had been a
very new house surgeon. Now she was beginning to
know the ropes. All anaesthetists sounded cross when

roused from sleep and told there was an emergency operation to do, likewise pathology technicians when asked to cross-match blood at four in the morning. Even Peter, the ebullient and friendly, who spent half the night drinking tea in the ward kitchens of his favourite night nurses, could be grumpy if called out of bed just before dawn, as they had been tonight.

'It's the worst time,' he grumbled. 'When we've finished it'll hardly be worth going back to bed.'

'Then you should go early when you have the chance,' retorted Jill.

'Early' meant well after midnight when you were first on call, but Jill had found that even a few hours' sleep then was a bonus worth having. They were sitting in the surgeons' room waiting for the anaesthetist to arrive, because the anaesthetic houseman wasn't experienced enough to deal with a major operation.

'I'm a night bird myself,' Peter commented, 'I never go to bed before two.'

The theatre block was on the top floor of Q.C.H. Jill, wearing her theatre clothes of white dress, headscarf and rubber shoes, leant her arms on the windowsill and pressed her nose to the cold windowpane. Already a few lights were coming on in blocks of flats, and there was a thin but steady stream of cars down the main road, which lay only a hundred yards or so from the hospital.

'London never really sleeps, does it! Don't you think life's exciting in a big city?'

'It's exciting all right,' Peter agreed with an unusual touch of dryness. 'Though that poor kid with the stab wound might not agree with you. How is he, by the way?'

'Doing all right now. The last of the blood's running in.' Jill had just come from the ward, and had been relieved to see that the waxen pallor of almost total exsanguination had gone at last. The boy would live, and the police would take a statement from him as soon as his surgeons gave them the go-ahead.

Peter had never operated on a lacerated liver before, and had called on the R.S.O. for help and advice. In some teaching hospitals the R.S.O.'s functions were mainly administrative, but at Q.C.H. he took an active part in surgical work. In less than a week the R.S.O. would be starting his study leave and Luke would be taking over from him.

Absorbed in the routine of her demanding job, Jill had forgotten all about Luke for a few days. Now, remembering, she asked Peter if he would mind taking orders from his brother.

Peter stared. 'Why should I? Old Luke's a damn good surgeon, and a whole lot more experienced than I am.'

'More experienced than the R.S.O.?'

'Yes, I should say so. He's looking around for a senior registrar's job. This will only be a stopgap.'

'The R.S.O. will be away three months. Will your brother leave before then if something better turns up?' Jill asked hopefully.

Peter's brows drew together in a frown that made him look, for one moment, astonishingly like his grandfather. 'Don't you think you're being rather silly about my brother? If you don't like him, keep out of his way. It shouldn't be that difficult, because he won't mix much with the junior residents anyway.'

The R.S.O. sat at the head of the registrars' table at meal-times, and he had his own self-contained flat on the first floor of the residency. Jill had only been in it once, when summoned there for a dressing down. Not a very severe dressing down, because she was conscientious and hard-working. Just a cool reminder that it wasn't the thing to invite students into the residents' common room. The rigid hierarchy of a teaching hospital had to be maintained for the sake of discipline. The students who were living in, while on their obstetric course, had their own quarters.

The R.S.O. ruled the residents with an iron hand, and some of Jill's friends made no secret of their pleasure at his imminent departure. But remembering Luke Haddon's air of tough efficiency, Jill doubted if they would find the change for the better.

November the first was a Tuesday, which meant a morning in Theatre, a snatched lunch and an afternoon in Out-patients, which went on longer than it might have done, because Sir James enjoyed teaching. When the last patient had been examined, when the students had departed and Sir James had had his ritual cup of tea with Sister Brown, his hard-worked juniors were free to depart.

They took the short cut, leaving by the Out-patients exit and crossing the small side street that separated the main hospital block from the residency. It was nearly dark now and the street lights were on. Under her white coat Jill wore a thin dress, because Out-patients was always overheated. She shivered in the cold autumn air, and ran up the steps to the front door ahead of the others.

The dining-room was to the left of the main hall. When she opened the door the first person she saw was Luke. He sat at the registrar's table, deep in conversation with the man he was replacing. He didn't look up, and Jill slipped into a vacant seat so that she had her back to him. Peter might call her silly, but there was something about the man that roused a quite unusual degree of hostility in her. She had always considered herself easy to get on with, and not given to make snap judgments about others, and Luke was the only person she could remember whom she had disliked practically on sight.

Above the chatter of her colleagues she caught Peter's cheerful exclamation, 'Hallo, Luke! Are you starting straight away?' and the R.S.O.'s relieved reply,

'He's already begun, Haddon. At four o'clock exactly I went off duty, and believe me, you two, working for the M.S. will be a rest cure compared with running this place!'

The M.S. stood for Master of Surgery. Luke already possessed it, along with a formidable array of other qualifications. It would have been nice to dismiss him as a swot, who had a slick examination technique; there were quite a few of that type around, but Luke it appeared wasn't one of them. He coupled academic brilliance with a gift for surgery, and a diagnostic flair unusual in so young a man. In the last few days Jill had grown tired of hearing about the wonderful Luke Haddon.

He was speaking now, his deep voice amused. 'I expect I'll survive. Did the work get you down, or the residents?'

'Both,' said the R.S.O. succinctly, and added after a moment, 'They're an unruly bunch and need a firm hand.'

'They'll get that from Luke,' commented Peter, and raised his voice quite unnecessarily, since most of the residents were already listening avidly. 'Hear that, you lot? The boss says you're out of hand!'

There were only a few young doctors left at the bottom table. In the manner of hospital meals people came and went very quickly. Jill's friend Gwyneth, who was sitting opposite her, gave a cheeky grin and launched into a pert rejoinder. The R.S.O., mellowed perhaps by the thought of his new-found freedom, forbore to make a caustic reply. He left a minute or two later and Gwyneth, who liked to clown, was now well away, saying that since they had such a bad reputation anyway, they had nothing to lose. 'So join me in a sitdown, boys and girls. We're overworked and underpaid——'

'Do shut up, Gwyneth!' That was Bill Mackie, the

other house surgeon on Sir James' team, a serious-minded Scot who found Gwyneth's Welsh vivacity a little hard to take.

'I will not shut up!' Gwyneth exclaimed indignantly. 'I've had years of being pushed around as a medical student. I thought things would be different when I qualified.'

She was only half joking, for Gwyneth was a great one for her rights. During their training days she had been a leading light of the students' union, a compulsive marcher and protester, especially in the more outrageous political causes.

'Things *are* different,' a dry voice commented from just behind Jill. 'They're tougher, for one thing. If you can't stand the pace why take up medicine?'

Jill turned slowly in her chair. The Haddon brothers had left their table and had paused for a moment on their way out. Peter was registering amusement, but Luke, hands in the pockets of his white coat, just stood there unsmiling, eyeing Gwyneth with grim disfavour. The Welsh girl coloured under that steady stare.

'I was only joking,' she muttered defensively, and Luke gave a brisk nod.

'Glad to hear it. How about a few introductions, Peter? Miss Bentley'—the cool gaze transferred to Jill—'I already know, of course.'

So Peter introduced the others, and Luke was courteous but distant. Gwyneth, her colour still high, made herself scarce, a half-eaten cake left on her plate. Luke didn't seem in a hurry to go. In fact when Bill asked if he would like another cup of tea, he sat down beside Jill and talked rugby with the men.

Pride stopped Jill from following Gwyneth out. She was hungry and she wasn't going to allow the wretched man to drive her away. She ate steadily, looking straight ahead of her, only half listening to Bill giving a blow-by-blow account of the last match Q.C.H. had played. Rugby was so boring if you hadn't been brought up to it, as girls with brothers were. Unconsciously she sighed, and Luke turned towards her.

'Not interested in Rugger, Miss Bentley?'

'Not really.'

'Gwyneth's crazy about it,' Peter remarked. 'Comes of her Welsh blood, I suppose.'

'Gwyneth? Oh, the little girl who was showing off just now.' Luke's tone was contemptuous and Jill leapt to her friend's defence.

'Gwyneth wasn't showing off. She gets carried away.'

'You can say that again!' murmured Bill.

'And,' Jill persisted doggedly, 'she doesn't mean half she says. Don't you agree, Peter?'

But Peter, so often her ally, wasn't prepared to back her up now. 'If she doesn't mean it she shouldn't say it. Personally I find her a pain in the neck.'

'Me too,' agreed Bill, and Jill scowled at them both.

'Why do men always gang up? But you can't deny the girl's good at her work.'

Peter shrugged and the Scotsman put on what Jill called his stolid look. Luke intervened. 'They don't seem to like your little friend, Miss Bentley. For that matter neither did I. She sounded a born trouble-maker.'

'No, she's not,' Jill denied hotly, 'but she does believe in a fair deal for junior doctors.'

'So she's one of them,' Luke said with distaste. 'More interested in medical politics than in medicine.'

Bill gave a nod of assent at the same moment that Jill shook her head angrily. 'That's a very sweeping statement, Mr Haddon. You've scarcely exchanged a dozen words with the girl.'

'And don't want to,' he said dismissively. 'Do you think we might drop the subject, Miss Bentley?' He turned to Peter. 'Shall we go round the wards now? I'd like to see what the bed state is.'

The R.S.O. was responsible for accepting emergency admissions, and needed to have an exact idea of the number of empty beds. As they went out Bill raised an eyebrow at Jill. 'I'm thinking this one may be worse than the last,' he observed. 'If you're wise, young Jill, you won't tangle with him.'

'He's so unreasonable,' Jill muttered, crumbling the remains of her cake in disgust.

'I'd say the man has strong views.'

'I'd say he was prejudiced and narrow-minded.'

'Could it be that you're a wee bit prejudiced your-self?' Bill asked mildly, and Jill agreed rather ruefully that he might well be right.

Greatly to her surprise Gwyneth didn't echo her senti-ments about Luke. The Welsh girl, who was usually so prickly towards her seniors, seemed to admire his force-ful personality.

'He's quite a man, isn't he? I'll bet no one pushes *him* around!'

'Correct! He does the pushing.' Jill lay back in the one comfortable armchair in her room, while Gwyneth sprawled inelegantly on the bed.

'He's quite a man,' the other girl repeated, and Jill gave her friend a disgusted look.

'For heaven's sake, Gwyneth! Haven't you any pride? He was thoroughly disagreeable and you know it.'

'Oh, well.' Gwyneth dismissed that with a wave of her hand. 'I asked for it in a way.' She smiled to herself. 'I shall toe the line when he's around, won't you?'

Her reaction, when Jill thought about it, was fairly predictable. Gwyneth was fiery, emotional and very feminine; she enjoyed arguments but despised people who let her win one. She was clever but not very sens-ible. She was, in short, thoroughly mixed up, but ex-tremely lovable, though on the whole she got on better

with her own sex than with men. It was to be hoped
that she wouldn't develop one of her violent but mercifully short-lived crushes for their new R.S.O.

They were so busy that week, even though they
weren't on emergency take, that Jill hardly saw Luke
except once or twice in the dining-room. Peter was
more than competent and only needed to call on his
brother in a grave emergency. There were less experienced registrars on some of the other firms, so presumably Luke was fully occupied in offering them the
benefit of his own wide experience. A week slid by and
Jill had come to accept his presence, was indeed hardly
aware of his existence. Then one evening, when she
was sitting over a late supper with some of the other
residents, Luke walked into the dining-room accompanied by one of the junior registrars, and a houseman
from the same surgical firm.

He stopped by their table. 'I want a couple of
volunteers for Theatre. A bad road accident—two
people with multiple injuries, and not much to pick
between them, so we plan to run two theatres at once.
Anyone free?'

Three of the young doctors there were house physicians. That left Bill Mackie, Jill and another houseman who had just been summoned on the telephone
to put up a blood transfusion. 'I've something to do on
the wards, Mr Haddon.' His respectful manner irritated Jill. The new R.S.O. was after all only a few years
older than they were.

Luke's eyes went to Bill. 'You free, Mackie? And
you, Miss Bentley?'

Bill nodded, and Jill said that yes, she supposed she
was. In an emergency you lent a hand, even if it
wasn't strictly speaking your night on call. She had
thought that she might pop round to the cinema
which stood on the next corner to Q.C.H. The last per-

formance would be starting shortly, and an obliging manager kept special seats for the young residents, so that they could easily be called out if required.

'Bang goes my evening off,' Jill said resignedly, and Luke, who had turned towards the door, swung back again. 'You're off duty, Miss Bentley?' He rapped the words out so sharply that Jill's hands clenched nervously.

'N-not really. I just felt like a break at the cinema. But of course I'll help if you need me.'

'Right. Main theatre at nine sharp. And Miss Bentley, I don't expect the residents to go out when they're on call.'

'Oh.' Jill digested this and would have been wiser to remain silent. But wisdom seemed to desert her when Luke Haddon was around. 'Mr Fowler didn't mind, as long as we told switchboard where we were.'

Luke's lips compressed. 'I am not,' he said softly, 'Mr Fowler.'

'I know, but——'

'I haven't time to argue with you, Miss Bentley!' he said curtly, jerked his head at the other registrar and left the room.

Bill pursed his lips and shook his head at Jill. 'You can't win, my girl. More sensible not to try.'

Jill had a patient to examine for tomorrow's operating list. She guessed that she might be a long time in Theatre, so decided to go to the women's ward straight away. An hour should have been plenty of time, but the patient was old and deaf, and had a sheaf of case notes as thick as an encyclopaedia. Jill was still ploughing through them when the telephone rang in the little office. She answered it and Bill spoke. 'Come on, Jill, we're just about to begin!'

Dismayed, Jill raced down the long corridor to the lift, but the lift was on the top floor and showed no sign of descending when she put her finger on the bell.

She took the wide stairs two at a time, nearly knocking down the Night Superintendent, who shook her head disapprovingly and would certainly have stopped her if she had been a nurse instead of a doctor.

The female house surgeons changed with the nurses. Jill took a minute or two to find a clean theatre dress, and her own pair of white shoes. She was still pushing her long black hair up under her headscarf as she went down the main theatre corridor.

She hoped she would be working with the other registrar and not with Luke, but she was out of luck. The others were nearly ready, the registrar and Bill already gloved and gowned. Luke stood impatiently while a little nurse, who scarcely reached his shoulder, tied the tapes on the back of his gown.

'Hurry up, Miss Bentley! You'll be working with me.'

He strode off in the direction of the theatre, where another house surgeon was laying sterile towels on the patient. By the time Jill arrived Luke had already made the first incision, for they feared multiple internal injuries and speed was essential. The house surgeon who was really first on call that night acted as first assistant, so as second assistant Jill had plenty of time to watch Luke at work. By the end of that long and gruelling operation she was sure of one thing; the people who said he was a brilliant surgeon were correct. If he was a fast-rising star in the tough world of the teaching hospitals it was on merit, and not because he had the right connections.

The anaesthetist confirmed her opinion. 'Good thing you were on tonight, Haddon, or that young woman might not have pulled through.'

She had been a front seat passenger, and had received ghastly internal injuries. She would suffer a stormy convalescence, but her chances of total recovery were very good. She owed her life to Luke's skill, and since she was under thirty, with three young children, it was a very precious life indeed.

Luke shrugged off the compliment, asked the other house surgeon to check on the patient's condition before he changed, and paused in the doorway of the surgeons' room for a word with Jill. 'Thanks for your help, Miss Bentley, and sorry to keep you out of bed.'

He was being quite decent, and the smile he gave her was a very nice one. If she didn't watch out she would end up like Gwyneth, and capitulate completely to him. For in the white shirt and trousers that all the surgeons wore he was undeniably attractive, and made more so by that air of self-assurance that all the best surgeons seemed to have. They were the aristocrats of the medical world and knew it, none better! Jill thought that Luke was probably very conceited, and only too aware of the stir he caused among his female colleagues.

She said politely that she'd been glad to help, but didn't mention that far from going to bed she would have to spend another half hour on the wards, finishing off her case notes for tomorrow. When she finally made her way back to the residents' quarters it was nearly two. A light still burned in the common room, so she looked in to see if any of her friends were there. The big room was deserted apart from Luke, who sat in front of the fire, his long legs stretched out and a newspaper on his knees. She would have backed out without saying anything, but he must have seen her out of the corner of his eye, for he looked up in surprise.

'Still up, Miss Bentley? Why don't you go to bed while you have the chance?'

'I had something to do on the wards.' She hung there in the doorway for a moment, less poised than usual because that was the effect Luke had on her. She was just about to say goodnight, when he asked if she'd like a cup of tea.

'I've only just made it, so come and join me.'

The sooner she conquered this absurd feeling of awkwardness the better, since she had to work with the wretched man and was not going to let him see how he disturbed her. 'Thank you,' she said, and went into the kitchen off the common-room to fetch another cup. When she returned Luke had opened up the front of the big stove and poked the fire into a blaze.

'This was here in my grandfather's day. They tried to remove it when I was a house surgeon, but we all kicked up such a fuss that in the end they left it.'

The old-fashioned stove gave out a magnificent glow, and was more comforting in the middle of the night than radiators. Jill drew her chair closer, sipped tea and left it to Luke to make conversation. He flipped his newspaper on to a table and stretched his hands out to the blaze. His fingers were long and flexible, delicate yet strong, the fingers of a surgeon or a musician.

'Do you play anything?' Jill asked suddenly, and he stared at her. 'I mean, a musical instrument.' She drank tea to hide the shyness she felt when he looked at her.

'I play the clarinet, but I don't get much time these days.' He lay back in his chair and closed his eyes, and she noticed for the first time that the Californian tan was fading rapidly. He looked in fact quite drawn with tiredness, so why didn't he too go to bed?

When she asked him he opened his eyes and said that he would in a few minutes, but first he wanted to have a final check on the young woman they had just operated on. He talked surgery for the next few minutes, and totally absorbed, Jill forgot to be shy. She also forgot that she didn't like him. She had shared in a very minor way in the saving of a life. They had worked together, and the experience had inevitably broken down some of the barriers between them. Perhaps Luke felt this too, for when they parted at the door of the common-room he gave her a singularly attractive smile, and said that he hoped she would be able to have a lie-in in the morning.

A lie-in would have been very welcome, but unfortunately it wasn't possible. Today was Sir James' biggest operating day, when they ran two theatres, with the great man in one and Peter in the other. Sir James' list finished at four o'clock, but Peter still had one more patient.

'I picked the wrong team,' Jill sighed, looking enviously after Bill's stocky figure as he vanished through the swing doors at the end of the corridor.

'And I thought you preferred working with me!' Peter joked. He flung a friendly arm around her shoulders and she smiled up at him.

'Sometimes I do, especially on the old man's off days.'

'So you're coming round to my view at last?'

'Well, Sir James can be horribly pompous——'

Someone pushed open the door of the surgeons' room, and Jill broke off in mid-sentence. Luke came in, wearing a dark suit and the crimson fellowship tie. He looked distinguished and decidedly disapproving, though whether that was because he had seen Peter's arm around Jill, or because of her indiscreet remarks, she wasn't sure. Perhaps both, because he said drily that it was a good thing it had been himself and not Sir James.

'The old man's deaf,' said Peter airily, took in Jill's red face and laughed. 'You know you agree with her, Luke, so don't be stuffy.'

Luke opened his locker and fished out his theatre clothes. 'Do you mind, Miss Bentley? I want to get changed.' Gone was the friendliness of last night as if it had never been.

'Her name's Jill,' remarked Peter, glancing from his brother to his young house surgeon. 'You'll be seeing a good deal of her from now on, so for God's sake drop the formality.'

Luke swung his theatre clothes in his hand and looked thoughtful. 'Is that so? Then perhaps, my dear Jill'—he put his hands on her shoulders and turned her towards the door—'you'd be so kind as to let me get changed. I've an emergency in ten minutes.' He pushed the door to behind her, but it didn't quite shut, and as she went into the nurses' room she heard his next remark. 'I didn't realise you were serious about that girl.'

Then Peter's reply, cut off in mid-sentence as the door swung to behind her. 'I think you'll agree——'

She was puzzled by Luke's words until she remembered Peter's rather ambiguous remark, that Luke would be seeing a good deal of her in the future. He had meant in the hospital, presumably, though Luke could have interpreted it differently, especially in conjunction with that friendly hug, which had been just that—friendly, not amorous. Peter liked big blondes; Jill was most definitely not the type of girl in whom he usually showed an interest. Luke must have forgotten what his brother was like. He probably put his arm round a dozen girls during the course of one day!

As if to prove her wrong Peter did start showing an interest in her, taking her out for the odd meal on their nights off, sometimes on their own, more often with another couple. The night they went to the theatre, however, it was just the two of them, and afterwards they walked back to the hospital arm in arm. Q.C.H. wasn't far from the West End and it hadn't been worth taking Peter's car, because of the inevitable parking problems. He had suggested a taxi, but Jill had sniffed the frosty air, looked up at the clear star-strewn sky, and said she'd prefer to walk.

They swung along gaily, laughing and talking, arguing about the comedy they had just seen, relaxed and happy. In the hall of the residency they met Luke, talking to one of the medical registrars. Peter raised a casual hand to his brother and would have gone past, but Luke stopped him. 'Hang on a moment. I want a word with you.'

While he finished what he was saying to the medical registrar his eyes travelled slowly over Jill. She was sparkling with health and vivacity, her cheeks pink, her eyes shining. It had been the walk that had made her look like that, but it could equally well have been Peter. Luke smiled. As the registrar turned away he commented, 'You're looking very pretty, Miss Bentley. Jill,' he amended, the smile becoming sardonic.

Discomfited by that smile, Jill would have left them, but Peter tucked her hand through his arm and held on to it. 'Cut it short, Luke. Jill and I want a hot drink to warm us up.'

'Then come along to my flat.' As they mounted the stairs to the first floor he added in his brother's ear, 'Was it cold in the park?'

Jill's quick ears picked up this remark and she blushed, because she knew what he was thinking. Regent's Park was only a few hundred yards from the hospital and much favoured by amorous residents. Probably Peter had taken a good many girls there over the years, medical students, nurses, the lot! Luke could be forgiven for assuming that his brother's present interest in Jill was following the familiar pattern.

Even so, it was irritating to be labelled one of Peter's girls when she so definitely wasn't. He treated her as a friend, nothing more. He had shown no inclination to kiss her when they were walking through the deserted back streets just now. If Jill had been a different sort of girl she would have been piqued. As it was she was relieved, because though she liked him very much, she wasn't in the least attracted to him. It was better this way when they worked together.

'I don't think I'll come in,' murmured Jill. 'I'm sure you'd rather talk on your own.'

'Don't be shy,' said Peter, and Luke stood back politely so that she could walk past him. She went in, and while Luke made coffee he talked to Peter. It appeared that Mrs Haddon was mildly annoyed with her younger grandson for neglecting her lately.

'She says it's ages since you've even telephoned. I told her,' said Luke, turning round and giving Jill an appraising stare, 'that your mind was probably on other things. Anyway, she hopes you'll go down on your next free weekend.' He handed Jill a cup of coffee, then sat down beside her. Jill shifted in her chair, because try though she might she never could relax in his company.

Peter was working out his next weekend off. 'It's the one after next, isn't it, Jill? Like to go down to Sussex again?'

Jill felt uncomfortable. Mrs Haddon had been kind and welcoming, but she saw so little of Peter. She would surely prefer him on his own?

'Thank you, but—but perhaps I ought to go home.' It was only an excuse, and Peter treated it as such.

'You told me you hated going home. Come on, Jill, you know you enjoyed yourself last time.'

'You don't get on with your family, Jill?' Luke asked quietly.

'I——' she couldn't possibly tell Luke the things she had told Peter, and now she regretted telling him.

Peter cut in with his own version. 'She has a wicked stepmother. And a stepsister, though I don't know if she's ugly. Is she, Jill?'

Jill coloured and avoided Luke's sardonic gaze.

'Please drop it, Peter. Your brother isn't interested in my affairs.'

It was one of Peter's faults that he didn't know when to stop. 'But I'm interested. You didn't say much about your sister. Do you dislike her too?'

'I don't exactly dislike either of them,' Jill said flatly. 'I just don't feel ... at home with them.' She gave a little sigh, which she instantly regretted when Luke spoke.

'Cinderella Bentley! How convenient that there's a prince around.' He said it jokingly, but though his mouth smiled his eyes didn't. He thought she was playing on Peter's sympathy and he despised her for it.

She drained her coffee cup and stood up. 'I'm tired. I think I'll go to bed.'

'Hold on,' said Peter, 'are you coming or not?'

'I'll let you know later. Thanks for the coffee, Mr Haddon.'

'Luke would be more friendly,' Peter suggested. His brother said nothing, merely crossed the room to open the door for her. As she drew level with him he looked down at her.

'I shall be on duty that weekend, if that's why you're hesitating.'

Jill had had enough of Luke Haddon and his digs. She put her head back and met his eyes squarely. 'It's of no interest to me where you'll be, Mr Haddon.'

Peter made a surprised sound. 'What goes on, you two? That sounded nasty, Jill.'

'It was meant to be nasty,' Jill said defiantly, 'but so was your brother's remark.' She stalked through the door, head high, but her exit was spoilt when she tripped and nearly fell. Luke's hand shot out to steady her. It was a maddening little incident, made worse by the fact that he was laughing at her. He had shut the door of the flat before she reached the end of the corridor.

As she stood with her thumb on the bell of the lift, Jill decided that she would go down to Medhurst with Peter, and let Luke make what he liked of it. The lift clanged to a halt and she stepped inside, slamming the doors with quite unnecessary violence, which was unusual for her, since she was generally a quiet girl.

CHAPTER THREE

JILL's second visit to the Haddons was, from her point of view at any rate, more successful than the last. To begin with she was expected and secondly Luke was not there. And finally any shadow of doubt about her welcome was swept away by Mrs Haddon's reception. They arrived late on Friday night, having eaten before they left London. The Professor had already gone to bed.

'Doctor's order's,' Mrs Haddon explained, 'because his blood pressure was higher than it should be. 'Now sit by the fire, my dears, and tell me all your news.'

Next morning Professor Haddon took Jill to see his greenhouse, an honour reserved for the favoured few, as Peter informed her afterwards. In the evening the old man played chess, first with his grandson and then with Jill, when he realised that she had been taking more than just a polite interest in the game.

On Sunday they all went to church, where they met the Henderson parents, but not Shirley, for which Jill was thankful. The girl would have been put out to see Jill down again so soon, and it might have been more difficult this time to convince her that Peter wanted nothing more than friendship. For that matter Jill was beginning to have difficulty in convincing herself on that point.

The Haddons seemed to assume that she was Peter's steady girl-friend, and they had begun to treat her almost as one of the family. It was very flattering to be accepted by them, but it made her a little uneasy, the more so as Peter was obviously delighted by his grandparents' open approval.

'They like you,' he announced, when they were walking in the grounds after Sunday lunch. The

49

weather wasn't sunny as on their last visit. In fact there was a freezing mist, which had made them give up the idea of a longer walk.

'I like them too,' Jill smiled, and dug icy hands into the pockets of her coat. 'Peter, couldn't we go inside?'

'I plan to do just that.' He slid a hand through her arm, guided her down a yew walk and pulled her into a small summer-house at the end of it. When he shut the door it was fractionally warmer, but almost as dark. Jill put out her hands as he bumped into her.

'Why in here? Why not——'

He tipped her hood back from her face, pulled her into his arms and kissed her with the expertise of much practice. Jill was taken completely by surprise, though she shouldn't have been; Peter's behaviour all weekend had clearly been leading up to this. He undid the toggles of her coat one by one and slipped his hands inside.

'Please, Peter! No!'

She jerked away from him breathlessly. A wooden bench ran along the wall of the summer-house. She sat down on it and said in a small voice, 'I'm sorry, but I wasn't expecting that.'

Some men might have been annoyed at being rebuffed, but Peter was amused. 'Jill dear, isn't it time you became a little more worldly? You're very sweet as you are, but you have to grow up some day.' He sat down beside her, put his arm round her shoulders and drew her towards him again. 'If we'd been anywhere but Grandma's house I'd have coming tapping on your door last night.'

Jill stiffened, but he wouldn't let her pull away. 'I'm sorry, Peter,' she repeated a little forlornly, 'but I didn't realise that's all you wanted.'

He stroked her silky dark hair, rubbed his cheek against it. 'If sex was all I wanted would I have brought you down here? I asked you down because you fit in so well, because my grandparents like you. Oh hell, because I wanted you around, I suppose.'

Jill laughed at that. 'Oh, Peter,' she said inadequately. 'Well, thank you at least for not pretending to be in love with me. Could we go back now?'

'No, we couldn't,' but he had relaxed his hold a little, and she rose quickly and started for the door, and in the half dark she didn't see an old chest in her path. She tripped over it, tried to save herself and fell heavily, twisting her ankle as she went down. The agonising pain made her feel sick and faint. She was hardly aware of Peter picking her up and carrying her outside, where the chill of the November air brought her round.

'Put me down,' she whispered, but when he lowered her carefully to the ground the pain and sickness returned.

In the end he carried her back to the house. In spite of the swelling Peter announced that in his opinion there was no fracture. The Professor agreed with him, but said that she must not go back to London tonight. She couldn't possibly work for a few days, so she had better stay on with them, and in addition she should have an X-ray in the morning, just to be on the safe side. Afraid of being a nuisance, Jill pointed out that she could rest in London, but Mrs Haddon backed up her husband. She would be no trouble. They had plenty of help in the house.

When Peter left, later than he had originally intended, he bent over the couch Jill was lying on, smiled and kissed her on the mouth. 'This wouldn't have happened if you'd been a bit more co-operative,' he said under his breath, and then more loudly, 'I'll come down on my next half day and take you back.'

Jill felt a little shy at this public kiss, but his grandparents watched with benign approval. They had already labelled her Peter's girl, and because they were old-fashioned she was sure they expected an engagement any day. Next afternoon when she was alone with Mrs Haddon, drinking tea out of exquisite white and gold cups, Peter's grandmother probed gently.

'You'll think I'm an interfering old woman, but I'm very fond of the boy. He needs to settle down with a nice girl like you.'

Jill tried, unsuccessfully, to convince Mrs Haddon that Peter wasn't seriously interested in her. That he had lots of girl-friends. That she liked him very much, but wasn't in the least in love with him.

Mrs Haddon smiled and nodded, and said that he had never brought another girl from the hospital home. Jill stared fixedly at the fire in the endeavour to keep a straight face, because she could see the funny side of it. Peter wanted an affair; marriage was most definitely not on his mind. Some of Jill's friends were promiscuous, but although she didn't condemn them, neither did she approve. She was old-fashioned enough to believe in love and want to wait until she found the right man.

The Haddons were charming to Jill and seemed to delight in spoiling her. She had breakfast in bed every morning, was taken for drives in the afternoon, 'To give you a change of scene. Young things get restless if they're stuck in the house.' She played chess in the evening with the Professor.

'You play well for a girl.' The old man was obviously not a believer in Women's Lib, but he enjoyed the company of a pretty and intelligent young woman, and Jill had rapidly discovered that the ferocious exterior concealed a warm and generous heart. He had probably terrified generations of students, she thought with amusement. There were legends about his ward rounds still, which she had only learnt since people knew she had met him.

Thursday had been fixed as the day when Peter would come down to collect her. He was expected about teatime, but the Haddons had a long-standing appointment which they were loath to break.

'Besides, Peter will be delighted to have you to himself for an hour or two,' Mrs Haddon remarked, when she came into the conservatory to say goodbye.

This was Jill's favourite spot on a sunny day. She stretched out on a cane lounger, because she had taken a short walk round the garden this morning and her ankle had started to ache again. She had daily papers, magazines, some books on gardening lent by the Professor, a box of chocolates given to her by Mrs Haddon. The conservatory was heated. Comfortable and drowsy, she amused herself in wondering what the others were doing at this moment, on Sir James' firm. It was one of their quieter afternoons, because the great man saw private patients, so the registrars took alternate half days on Thursdays. She hoped Peter wouldn't take advantage of the Haddons' absence to try and make love to her, and she decided to get up before he arrived, for she could get around quite well now with the aid of a stick.

Just half an hour more, she thought, closed her eyes and fell asleep. When she opened them again Luke stood at the foot of the lounger, hands in his pockets, with an expression that was difficult to read on his face. Jill lay for a few moments, too surprised to speak, while Luke's eyes roamed over the contents of the low table by her side, the magazines, the chocolates, the vase with a single late red rose which the Professor himself had picked for her. The unreadable expression became all too readable. When he looked back at her it was with sardonic amusement.

'You are being cosseted, aren't you? Sorry you've got to go back?'

'In a way,' Jill said steadily. 'Your grandparents have been very kind to me.'

'You mean they've spoilt you outrageously!'

'If you want to put it that way.' She swung her feet to the ground and reached for her stick. 'I didn't know you were coming down with Peter.'

'Change of plans.' He gave her a hand as she limped to the door. 'The other registrar has a virus infection, so Peter couldn't get away. I came instead.'

Jill digested this unwelcome news in silence, very conscious of his hand on her arm, and the tension she always felt when Luke was near her. She hadn't spoken to him since they had exchanged those sharp words at the door of his flat. Remembering them made her feel uncomfortable.

'Where are you going?' he asked, and she told him the drawing-room.

'Birdie said she'd bring tea there as soon as Peter arrived.' Birdie was the housekeeper. Jill had never heard her called anything else, so it slipped out quite naturally, but it made Luke quirk his eyebrows and whistle softly under his breath as they crossed the wide hall. He thought her presumptuous, assuming an intimacy with the family she didn't really have. Perhaps he thought that she had sprained her ankle on purpose, so that the Haddons would have to ask her to stay on! No, that was ridiculous. Even Luke couldn't believe that.

She limped into the drawing-room and took a seat by the fire, while Luke went to tell Birdie he had arrived. Tea came on an elaborately patterned silver tray which Jill thought too ornate, but the Georgian teapot and cream jug were beautiful. She felt diffident about offering to pour in case Luke took this as another example of her pushiness, so she felt aggrieved when he asked her, with thinly veiled sarcasm, if she had injured her wrist as well as her ankle.

Colour high, she snapped back at him, 'It's your house. I thought you might want to pour.'

He stretched out in his chair and stuck his feet on a small hassock. 'What a girl you are for losing your temper!'

So he had remembered that night at the residency. She poured tea with compressed lips, determined not to let him see how much he upset her. She passed his tea, helped herself to a scone and ate in silence, hoping that his grandparents wouldn't be late in returning.

Luke spoke at last. 'I've been thinking, my dear Jill'—even the way he said that set her teeth on edge— 'it's a pity we always seem to rub each other up the wrong way ... under the circumstances.'

Jill's hand stayed still, with the teacup half-way to her lips. 'Under what circumstances?' she asked warily.

'Peter and I have always been good friends. I'd rather it stayed that way.'

She still didn't follow his train of thought, and at her baffled expression he added impatiently, 'Peter won't like it if I quarrel with his girl.'

She said quickly, 'I'm not his girl. I wish everyone wouldn't jump to the wrong conclusion.'

'Everyone?'

'Well, your grandparents. Peter and I are just—just friends,' she finished weakly.

He handed her his cup for a refill. 'Peter doesn't seem to agree. In fact I'd say he was quite badly smitten.'

'No, he's not. You know how he is with girls.'

'Yes indeed, which is why I know he's serious about you. Why else would he bring you down here?'

Jill was getting a little tired of trying to explain. 'The first time it was just a casual invitation. This time——' she hesitated, then decided to speak bluntly. 'I wasn't going to come, but you made me mad, so I changed my mind.'

Luke was quick. He understood at once and gave a sharp smile. 'You surprise me, Jill. I should have expected you to jump at the invitation.'

'That's because you have a nasty suspicious mind, especially about me,' Jill told him coolly. 'You have a very cynical view of human nature, Mr Haddon.'

'Acquired through experience, Miss Bentley.' The mockery went, to be replaced by a brooding look. 'I was let down pretty badly once, by someone I trusted and admired. It's not pleasant ... to find you're being used.'

Someone he'd loved, when he was younger and more easily hurt? 'I'm sorry,' Jill said gently. 'But most people aren't like that.'

'A lot are.' He relapsed into silence again, and shortly afterwards his grandparents returned. They were surprised to find Luke instead of his brother, but pleased that he intended staying until quite late. 'If it's all right with you, Jill, we'll leave about ten. I could do with some home cooking after hospital meals!'

'I'm not at all sure,' Mrs Haddon worried, 'that Jill's ankle is really better. If she stayed until the week-end——'

'Grandma,' Luke said firmly, 'the girl is not a cripple. She can walk with a stick, and she has a job to do.' He spoke now as the R.S.O., with responsibility for the problems that arose if any of his juniors were off sick. Someone must have been doing extra hours on duty while Jill was away. She pointed that out to Mrs Haddon, and added that there was no question about it, she had to start work again tomorrow.

Mrs Haddon agreed reluctantly, saying how much they had enjoyed her company. 'And you look less tired for the rest, my dear. You must see that she isn't worked too hard, Luke.'

Luke's face was a study. In the end he laughed, and

a little uncomfortably Jill joined in. 'So you think the girl should have special consideration, Grandma? Might I ask why?'

'Because she's a girl, of course,' the old lady answered serenely, and Luke snorted.

'There's no sex discrimination in medicine. Women doctors have no right to expect an easier time than the men.'

'They don't,' Jill cut in quickly, and the Professor leant forward to pat her hand.

'I'm sure they don't, and Luke knows it too. He's merely being provoking.' A glare for Luke which that young man returned with an amused look. 'We understand why you have to go, but you must come again soon. Get Peter to bring you down the next time you're both free.'

'They've got you married off already,' Luke remarked, as they drove away from the house later that night. 'It's not a scrap of use insisting that Peter means nothing to you. My grandmother is a very determined old woman beneath that sweet exterior.'

'I am not marrying Peter just to please your grandparents! In the unlikely event of his asking me, that is.'

Luke took his hand off the wheel and tapped her lightly on the knee. 'I can't make you out, Jill Bentley. You sound sincere. Or perhaps you're just playing hard to get?' At her indignant gasp he laughed. 'Joke, my dear! Joke!' Only Jill didn't think it had been intended humorously.

Whatever Luke said about wanting to get on better with her for his brother's sake, he still didn't like her and most certainly didn't trust her. When they arrived back in London Luke helped her up the steps of the residency and accompanied her to the common-room. It was just on midnight and at this hour hot drinks and sandwiches were usually available. There were half a dozen people in the room, among them Gwyneth and Bill. Everyone stared as they came in, Luke with his hand through Jill's arm.

She limped to a chair and sat down. 'Hallo, it's nice to be back. Who's been coping with my work? You, Bill?' Bill nodded, and she said she was sorry to have been a nuisance, but she would make his extra time up as soon as she was more mobile.

'You won't be much good like that,' observed Gwyneth, and threw Luke a challenging glance. 'Why did you bring her back so soon, Mr Haddon?'

'Jill is perfectly fit to work,' Luke said evenly. 'It was only a sprained ankle.' He made it sound as if she needn't have been off at all, as if in his opinion it had all been a fuss about nothing.

Jill coloured and said under her breath, 'Drop it, Gwyneth, there's a dear. I shall be all right.'

Sir James Macaulay more than made up for Luke's lack of sympathy when he met her next day on his ward round. They waited for their chief in the main hall of Q.C.H., his registrars, his house surgeons and a bunch of students, for this was a teaching round, and Sir James was popular. Pompous he might be, but he was a shrewd judge of human nature, and to hear him questioning a patient was an education in itself. The hall porter swung open the double doors as Sir James' chauffeur drew up the gleaming grey Bentley opposite the entrance. Sir James climbed the steps, inclined his head to the porter, handed Peter his black bag and boomed a good morning to his assembled juniors.

Jill had relinquished her stick, not wanting to be conspicuous, but her limp was still pronounced and Sir James showed concern. 'You shouldn't have come back so soon, my dear child. You had better give my ward round a miss.'

It had to be that moment that Luke joined the crowd. He smiled to himself at Sir James' remark and murmured something in Peter's ear. 'I'm all right, Sir James,' asserted Jill. 'Honestly, I should hate to miss your ward round.' It was sincerely meant, for in Jill's opinion the Friday morning round was one of the high spots of the week.

Luke fell into place beside her as they moved off to the lift. 'Keep it up, Miss Bentley, and you'll have a grade A reference!'

She scowled at him, but before she could say anything Sir James beckoned them to his side. 'This child is too conscientious, Haddon. We're first on call this weekend, aren't we, but I don't want her overworked.'

'Sir James, I——'

'There must be someone who can stand in for her.'

'They've been standing in for her all week,' said Luke abruptly. 'We're short-staffed as it is, sir, with that virus infection spreading.'

'Ah yes, the virus infection,' Sir James rumbled as he entered the lift. 'Well, do your best, my boy, do your best.'

The lift only accommodated Sir James' firm and one or two visiting doctors. The students were in the habit of racing it to the third floor, where the ward round always started. Jill leant against the back wall of the lift to take the weight off her ankle, which was aching quite badly. When they reached the third floor she was slow to emerge and had to follow on behind the noisy mob of students, who had just clattered up the last flight of stairs. They went quicker than she did, so that by the time she entered Lister Ward everyone was grouped around a bed at the far end.

She limped down the ward, feeling rather self-conscious, watched sympathetically by the patients, among whom she was a general favourite. Old Mr Prior, who was first on the list for examination, gave a relieved grunt. He was frail, cantankerous and frightened, and Jill had promised to stand right beside him while Sir James held forth on his complaint.

'It ain't natural, miss, to have all those hands poking at you,' he had complained when Jill had told him earlier that morning about the forthcoming ward round.

She had sat on his bed and explained very earnestly how much it would help the students, because his complaint was a rare and interesting one. Mollified by the idea that he was someone very special, if only in illness, the old man had given way. Now he demanded in his thin quavering voice that Jill should stand close. Sir James beckoned her forward imperiously, and Mr Prior's bony old hand clutched at hers thankfully.

'They won't hurt, will they, doctor?' he muttered as Sister folded back the blankets expertly and undid his pyjamas.

Sir James, who was rubbing his hands together briskly, preparatory to laying them on Mr Prior's abdomen, gave an approving nod in Jill's direction. 'Miss Bentley has a real flair for handling nervous patients.' He was speaking to the visiting foreign surgeon who stood beside him, a dark stocky man with heavily greased hair and a clipped moustache above very white teeth. He smiled at Jill, looking her over very thoroughly as he did so.

'Such charm and expertise,' he murmured admiringly, in heavily accented but fluent English.

Jill blushed and stared at her feet, having intercepted the look of contemptuous amusement with which Luke Haddon viewed this little exchange. When they moved on to another patient the foreigner insisted on walking by her side, his hand under her elbow in case she should stumble. Gallantly he drew a chair forward. 'Sit, Miss Bentley, and save your poor injured leg.'

No one sat on ward rounds. Jill smiled a little desperately and shook her head. She compromised by holding on to the back of the chair, and taking the injured leg off the ground. Luke, who was right next to her, bent his dark head and spoke into her ear. 'You've done it again, Jill. Señor de Varga has an international reputation, as I'm sure you know.'

Jill pretended not to hear. Luke shrugged and drew away, but out of the corner of his mouth he added a warning. 'A good reputation for surgery and a bad one with women.'

The virus infection, which had been nibbling at the ranks of the medical staff, now struck with full force. By Saturday morning over half the residents were affected, and at breakfast Luke rapped on the table and delivered an ultimatum.

'Some of those who should have been off this weekend will have to stay on. I've put a revised duty roster on the notice board. Don't forget to look at it.'

Ankle apart, Jill was one of the healthy ones. So was Gwyneth, but neither Peter or Bill had come on duty this morning. Gwyneth grumbled as a matter of course. 'It's all right for you, Jill. You're on anyway, but I was going to watch the Harlequins this afternoon.' She had rushed out to study Luke's list and returned very disconsolate. 'I suppose,' she asked tentatively, 'YOU couldn't cope with my beds as well as your own? Just for a couple of hours.'

Gwyneth was rugby mad. Jill would have been pleased to oblige her, but was likely to be excessively busy herself, since Sir James' team was minus one of its registrars and one of its house surgeons. 'I wouldn't mind,' she said hesitantly, 'only I can't be in two places at once. What if I'm in Theatre and get an urgent call from the medical wards?'

She had spoken loudly because Gwyneth was a few places away at the table. Her remark was picked up by Luke, helping himself to coffee nearby. 'Why should

you get a call from the medical wards, Miss Bentley? I
haven't put you down for any medical duties.'

Jill muttered something into her teacup and Luke
crossed to their table with a frown. 'I hope you're not
trying to rearrange the duty roster for your own con-
venience?' He sat down opposite her, his face severe,
and the rest of the table watched with interest. Jill
threw an appealing look at Gwyneth. It had after all
been the Welsh girl's idea, but for once Gwyneth's
mouth stayed shut.

Luke stirred his coffee, sipped and spoke. 'Well, are
you or aren't you?'

Embarrassed, Jill shook her head. 'It—it was just an
idea.' Again she appealed to Gwyneth, but Gwyneth
was looking the other way. 'We—we wouldn't have
done anything without consulting you.'

'I'm relieved to hear it,' Luke said sarcastically, and
glared round the table. 'What are you lot gawping at?
Haven't you any work to do?'

The table emptied with almost comical speed. The
residents had been quick to learn that Luke, when
annoyed, had an abrasive tongue. 'Not you, my dear.'
Strong fingers closed round Jill's wrist as she started to
rise. 'I've accepted a couple of emergencies in the last
half hour. When you've examined them let me know.
I'll be in my room!'

'But ... what about Tim Barclay?'

Tim Barclay was the other registrar on Sir James'
firm, as quiet as Peter was lively, an earnest, rather
dull young man, who spent all his spare time in the
library.

'Barclay is in charge of the Accident Department for
the weekend,' replied Luke. 'Their usual registrar has
the bug too.'

So the bug was responsible not only for causing
havoc among the hospital staff, but for forcing Jill to
spend a lot more time in Luke's company than she

would normally have done. With Tim Barclay occupied elsewhere, she had no alternative than to consult Luke over any surgical problems, and was expected to assist him with all emergency operations. There were eight on that hectic Saturday, the last one a lad who had somersaulted over the handlebars of his motorbike. He required the combined attentions of Luke and the orthopaedic consultant, who had been called in because his registrar was also ill. The consultant remembered Jill from her student days and sat beside her in Sister's office, where they were drinking tea at the end of the operation.

'Tired, Miss Bentley? You should have joined my firm instead of Sir James'!'

The orthopaedic teams worked hard, but perhaps they had fewer post-operative complications to cope with than the general surgeons. Luke dropped into the chair on her other side and talked across her to the orthopaedic man. 'She wouldn't last a week in your game! You need muscle to reduce fractures and dislocations.' He picked up the girl's left hand, spread it out on his own palm. 'Look at that! Can you imagine young Jill pulling on the arm of a sixteen-stone rugger player?'

Jill had pretty hands, slim and white, with delicately shaped nails. The orthopaedic surgeon smiled at her. 'Don't let this lad bully you. I know what he can be like!'

Luke, it appeared, had done a six-month stint in orthopaedics before he left for the States. The older man seemed to like him, and the two surgeons were soon deep in an argument over some surgical problem, which was a relief to Jill since it diverted attention from herself. She had stiffened when Luke took her hand in his, and the blood had pounded in her ears in a most alarming way. He had only to look at her to make her tense up; when he touched her it was electrifying. No other man had ever affected her in this way, but then she had never disliked any other man quite so thoroughly.

The orthopaedic surgeon was leaving, thanking Sister Wyman for her hospitality. Jan sat behind the small table on which the tea-tray stood, wearing her white theatre dress. She had removed her headscarf, but her hair was still drawn back into the loose knot she wore on duty, and the rather severe style suited her. Luke very obviously approved of her and treated her as an old friend.

This was the first time Jill had seen them together, and she had no doubt about Jan's feelings for the new R.S.O. She lit up when he was around. She glowed when he spoke to her. Poor Jan, what a man to fall in love with! But at least he treated the young theatre Sister kindly, and thanked her warmly for her able assistance.

'I hope we won't meet again tonight,' he said with the charming smile that he never bestowed on Jill. 'This should have been your weekend off, shouldn't it?'

'And yours,' Jan reminded him a little breathlessly. 'I wasn't doing anything special. I was glad to lend a hand.'

The nursing staff were even more depleted than the residents. Jan said goodnight and went off down the corridor to see what her girls were up to. Luke asked, 'Had your supper, Miss Bentley? I didn't see you in the dining-room.'

There hadn't been time, because she had been called to the wards to put up a blood transfusion. When she said this Luke glanced at his watch. 'Ten o'clock. If they left anything for you it'll be uneatable by now. Come to my flat and I'll find something.'

'I don't think——'

'I'm not a bad cook.' He took her by the arm and

marched her off to the lift. 'Can't have you passing out for lack of food. We may have more work before the night's over.' He slammed the lift gates shut. 'It'd be too much to hope for a whole night in bed!'

Jill leant against the wall and stared at his profile. High forehead, strong nose, well-shaped lips, a forceful chin. He would be a distinguished old man, like his grandfather. He was a very striking-looking young one. He turned suddenly, eyebrows raised. 'Think you'll know me again next time?'

She straightened and spoke stiffly. 'I was just thinking ... how like your grandfather you are.'

'So I've been told,' he said casually, fished in the pocket of his white coat and waved a pink form at her. 'You forgot about that blood, didn't you?'

He had asked her earlier in the evening to send a specimen for a blood count, and Jill swallowed and muttered an apology. The lift came to a halt. 'Don't look so fraught,' he said pleasantly, 'I'll forgive you this time!'

They called in at the common-room and Luke presented the tube of blood, which he had taken himself, to the resident pathologist. The pathologist, who was filling in time with a game of bridge, pocketed the form and stuck the tube of blood in a plant pot. 'I'll do it before I go to bed.'

'Do it now,' Luke said sharply. 'It's urgent.' Surprising then that he hadn't torn strips off Jill for forgetting it, but perhaps eight emergencies in twelve hours excused a good deal. The pathologist looked annoyed, but rose without a word, throwing his cards on the table. Very few people argued with Luke these days.

'Sorry to break up your game, chaps,' he said. 'Come on, Jill.'

Off a corner of Luke's sitting-room was a minute kitchen. He produced eggs, a tin of mushrooms and a crusty French loaf. 'Will an omelette do?'

'Yes, thank you, but can't I make it?'

He piloted her to a chair, pushed her into it and stuck a stool under her foot. 'Rest while you can. You look all in. Is that ankle playing you up?'

'A bit.'

'I'll have a look at it after you've eaten.'

While he prepared her omelette Jill looked around; last time she had been here she had been too tense to notice anything. It was the regulation hospital room relieved by a few individual touches. Two rather nice etchings of London, several family photographs. She recognised his grandparents, though they looked quite a bit younger, and the middle-aged couple were presumably his parents. The very pretty blonde girl? She stared at it, caught Luke's eye and looked away quickly.

The omelette was mouth-watering, the bread delicious. Luke told her he bought it at the delicatessen on the corner. 'Now and then I feed myself, especially when I have friends in.' He picked up a bottle of red wine, looked at it thoughtfully and replaced it in the cupboard. 'Not tonight, I'm afraid, since you're on duty. Don't feel you have to make polite conversation.'

Which probably meant that *he* didn't want to, so Jill ate her meal with relish while Luke immersed himself in the *Journal of British Surgery*. He had remarkable powers of concentration, and she was sure he had forgotten all about her. A lock of thick dark hair fell in his eyes and he brushed it back impatiently. When the telephone pealed he stretched out a hand without looking up. 'Haddon here. You want who? Oh, Dr Bentley.' He passed the receiver to Jill.

It was Señor de Varga, the foreign surgeon she had met on yesterday's ward round, asking her to dine with him one evening. Jill was acutely conscious of Luke, who had lowered the surgical journal and was listen-

ing to every word. She was pretty sure that he knew
who it was. Flustered, she tried to think of an excuse,
but the man was very persistent. He knew how busy
she was, but any evening, positively any evening
would do. If Monday and Tuesday were no good, how
about Wednesday? Thursday?

'I can't plan that far ahead, Señor de Varga. No, I'm
sorry. Yes, I know, but——'

'I'll deal with him,' Luke said impatiently, and took
the receiver from her hand. 'Luke Haddon speaking—
the Residential Surgical Officer. Miss Bentley is far too
busy to meet anyone. We have a staff crisis on our
hands. I'm sorry, but I wouldn't excuse her from duty
for a royal command. Goodnight!' He quirked an eyebrow at her. 'That's how to do it. Be positive!'

'Positive?' Jill said weakly. 'I thought you were
rude.'

'Was I?' He didn't sound as if he cared. 'I didn't
take to that fellow. He could hardly keep his hands off
you on the ward round. I shudder to think what he'd
have been like if he'd got you alone somewhere.' Jill
blushed and he laughed rather unkindly. 'You should
have developed some sort of technique for giving unwelcome admirers the brush-off by your age. Or did I
misunderstand? Did you want to go out with him?'

'You know I didn't!' cried Jill indignantly. 'But I
don't like hurting people's feelings.'

'That sort can't be hurt,' he shrugged. 'They've too
good an opinion of themselves.'

'I suppose he has something to be conceited about.
He's a very great surgeon.'

'I know. Odd, isn't it,' Luke mused, busy with the
coffee pot, 'such a great man in his work and so unpleasant in his private life. When I was starting out in
medicine I assumed that all the top men had char-
acters to match their abilities.'

'Some do,' Jill argued. 'I'm sure your grandfather

has always been a man of integrity, both on and off
duty.'

'Well, I'm pretty sure he didn't make passes at
young girls,' Luke agreed with a grin. He must have
been as tired as she was, but it didn't show. He was one
of those people who thrive on hard work. In fact he
was in an excellent mood, and disposed for once to be
friendly. They lingered over coffee and when Jill said,
at last, that she must be going, he walked over to open
the door for her.

'If you've nothing to do on the wards, get to bed
while you can.'

'It's not worth it so early. We're bound to be called
out again.'

'An hour or two is always worth it.' He smiled down
at her with unusual kindliness. She was beginning to
think he wasn't so bad after all, when he spoilt it by
asking, 'Seen Peter today?' When she shook her head
he added drily, 'Wise girl. He's feeling very sorry for
himself, and in need of some comforting. A couple of
kisses and you'd have the infection too!'

CHAPTER FOUR

THE bug was no respecter of persons. It struck down Sir James with especial virulence, so that he would no longer be able to boast that he had never missed work through illness in his life. He asked Luke to take over for him on his teaching round, and the entrance hall was packed at ten o'clock. Luke had quite a reputation, and the students who hadn't met him were curious to find out why. He arrived on the stroke of ten, not through the front door, like Sir James, but by a side corridor, accompanied by a registrar. He raised his eyebrows at the crowd, but appeared in no way disconcerted by it.

Jill could not imagine Luke ever being shy or unsure of himself. A pretty girl student just behind her whispered to a friend, 'Is *that* Luke Haddon?'

The friend, who was plain but perky, giggled and nodded. 'If we stand right at the front perhaps he'll notice us,' she suggested hopefully.

They were so young! They made Jill feel old and mature. Had she ever sighed over attractive registrars as a student? If so, she couldn't remember. Smiling, she climbed the stairs with everyone else, for Luke disdained to use the lift.

The students expected fireworks on the ward round and they got them. Luke was a born teacher, with a clarity of thought and exposition that Jill had rarely heard equalled. He had in addition imagination and humour, and the combination was irresistible. Bill, standing beside her at the back of the crowd, murmured that the longer Sir James stayed away the better. 'I'd no idea he was this good.'

'I always knew he was very clever,' Jill agreed, but Bill dismissed her remark with scorn.

'Q.C.H. is stuffed with clever people. This chap has something extra.'

Over the heads of the students Jill caught Luke's eye. He stopped for a moment in mid-sentence and gave them a frown. It wasn't done to chatter on ward rounds; any moment now he would make one of his caustic comments. She retreated behind the broad form of the hospital's star rugger player, a final-year student whose brains didn't equal his physique. The young man's neck was still red from the grilling he had recently received at Luke's hands.

It was easy for an unkind teacher to make fools of his pupils, but Jill had noticed an endearing thing about Luke. It was only the brash and the cocky whom he cut down to size, and he was unexpectedly gentle with the shy and the awkward. The rugger forward had asked for it by being opinionated though ignorant.

The student who had clerked this case was in trouble. He had forgotten what the patient's blood chemistry showed, and Luke was asking which of the house surgeons was in charge. Jill, safely out of sight, had let her attention wander, but was brought back to the present by Luke's raised voice. 'Could you come out of that daydream, Miss Bentley, and give us the benefit of your knowledge?'

Sarcastic beast, she thought, as Bill stood aside to let her move forward. 'Er—what about, Mr Haddon?' She stammered and he let out a long sigh.

'This patient is under you, Miss Bentley? And you are interested in her? Good! Good! Then why aren't you paying attention?'

Several of the students tittered, relieved that the heat was off them. Red-faced, Jill said she was sorry but she hadn't quite caught the original question. Evenly Luke repeated it, but because she was flustered the information he wanted went out of her mind. She stammered. She swallowed, and then in despair, under his impatient and irritated gaze, she muttered that it would save time if she checked. The folder was a thick one, and there were pages of pathology reports. She flipped through them frantically, went back a second time.

'We haven't all day to wait,' snapped Luke, and took the file from her hands. He found it at once. He would, of course! A long forefinger stabbed the pathology form. 'Plasma proteins well below normal limits.' He swung back to the student. 'Now, why is that important?' and Jill was left to fade thankfully into the background again.

Bill gave her a sympathetic grin and a thumbs-up sign, but Jill was annoyed with herself for being found wanting. She prided herself on her efficiency, and if it had been dear old Sir James quizzing her she wouldn't have lost her head like that. It would be nice some day, she thought resentfully, to catch Luke out in a moment's inattention or absentmindedness, though the possibility seemed remote.

At the end of the round she lingered behind for a word with old Mrs Christie, who had no relatives at all to visit her, and whose present life had become centred on the ward. Jill looked at photographs of Mrs Christie's Canadian grandsons, and agreed, quite truthfully, that they were cute-looking kids. She listened to an extract from the latest air letter written by Mrs Christie's daughter-in-law, and didn't hear Luke come up behind her, so that she jumped when a hand came down on her shoulder.

'Come on, Miss Bentley. Have you forgotten about that child?'

He had said that he wanted to have a second look at a small girl with suspected appendicitis. 'Sorry, Mr Haddon, I thought you'd be having coffee first.'

'No time! There's a lot to do with so many people

away.' He looked thinner and older than he had done when she first met him, so perhaps even Luke could wilt a little under the strain.

Mrs Christie's small bright eyes darted from one to the other of them. 'You weren't very kind to this poor girl on the round, sir!' Mrs Christie was a cockney and quite irrepressible. She grinned at Luke and he grinned back at her. 'You made her nervous,' Mrs Christie reproved.

'Keeps her on her toes, Mrs C. Excuse us, please.' He strode off down the ward and took the stairs two at a time. He was undoubtedly very fit, and he reached the top several seconds ahead of Jill. He was leaning against the wall, watching with amusement as she panted up the last few stairs. 'You're out of training, my girl. Do you ever take any exercise?'

In the course of a day she probably walked several miles up and down stairs, and along the corridors and underground linking tunnels of the vast hospital. When she pointed this out Luke shrugged and said disparagingly that it wasn't what he called exercise. 'Do you ever play squash?'

'Tennis in the summer. Squash is too fast for me.'

Peter had told her that his brother had been the inter-hospitals champion in the old days, besides being a very useful bat in Q.C.H.'s cricket team. There must be something he was bad at, though Jill hadn't yet discovered it.

That evening, when she called to see Peter, he asked her how she was getting on with Luke.

'I gather you're practically the last two survivors on the surgical side.'

'Bill's back, but he looked so peaky after a day on the wards that I told him to go home.'

'You're looking a bit tuckered yourself.' Peter patted the side of his bed. 'Sit down, I'm not infectious now, though Dr Milstein won't allow me up till tomorrow.'

He had a two-day growth of beard, which gave him a faintly raffish appearance, and the fresh complexion was a little less clear than usual. Even so he looked very attractive in bright blue pyjamas that exactly matched his eyes. Endearing was the word for Peter. It was not a word you would ever use for his brother, Jill thought inconsequentially, and felt a flash of irritation because she so often seemed to think of Luke these days.

Peter punched his pillows irritably and Jill leant forward to pile them more comfortably. When she tried to draw away he wouldn't let her, pulling her into his arms and running his lips down her smooth cheek. His own skin was bristly and abrasive.

'No, Peter. Peter, please——'

'You talk too much,' he murmured, turned her face firmly towards him and kissed her full on the lips.

'Very unhygienic,' commented a dry voice from the door. Luke had just come in and was standing watching them, with what Jill thought of as his superior expression. She jerked out of Peter's arms and brushed back her long dark hair.

'Nothing unhygienic about it,' Peter protested. 'It's only a twenty-four-hour infection.'

'Then why aren't you on your feet, you lazy so-and-so?' Luke asked, and Jill leapt quickly to the defence.

'Because he's still convalescent. Surely you can see how unwell he looks? This virus is a beastly one and has taken a lot out of him.'

'Yes, doctor,' said Luke with unusual mildness.

'I'm serious. Poor Bill was completely flaked out by the end of the day.'

'So she's sent him home to the arms of his loving wife, and she's standing in for him tonight. A good sport, our Jill,' Peter said approvingly.

Luke gave her a searching look. 'When did you last

have a night off yourself? The end of last week, wasn't it?'

Not since he'd brought her back to London in fact, but then neither had he. When she pointed this out he brushed it aside. 'I can do without much sleep, but you're beginning to show the strain.' The rather hard face softened a little. 'Perhaps I shouldn't have grilled you on the ward round the way I did.'

'You weren't very nice,' Jill agreed ruefully, and he laughed.

'Then I apologise, my dear. Look, surely there's someone else who can cover tonight?' He pulled a small notebook from his pocket and consulted it. 'Damn! There isn't. Well, when this lazy bunch are back at work you and I will take a few days' holiday.'

'Together?' Peter asked, eyebrows comically raised, and Luke's answering smile was sardonic.

'I don't think Jill would consider it a holiday if I was around.' *And nor would I*, hung in the air, though he didn't say it.

In the end the few days off were whittled down to two nights when she wasn't on call, and the day in between. Doctors were expected to undertake extra duties in an emergency. If you were young and healthy you should be able to make up for lost sleep very quickly. On her night off Jill fell into bed at eight-thirty, told herself it would be impossible to sleep for hours because the residents were so noisy, laid her head on the pillow and went out like a light.

She only woke when a smiling maid brought her breakfast in bed. This was an unexpected treat. Jill blinked and stared. 'Oh, Sophie, you are kind! What a luxury!'

Sophie, who was middle-aged and motherly, admitted that it hadn't been her idea but Mr Haddon's.

'As if you haven't had enough trouble running up

and down stairs after him and the other invalids.' Jill poured tea and sipped happily.

Sophie smiled benignly. 'Not Mr Peter Haddon, miss. The other one.'

It took Jill a moment or two to get her meaning. 'Luke!' she exclaimed. 'You mean *Luke* Haddon asked you to bring my breakfast?' The idea was truly astonishing.

'Yes, of course, miss. Now there's a real gentleman,' Sophie said admiringly. 'Asked me ever so nicely if it would be too much bother. Said you needed a bit of cosseting after the last few days.'

The idea of Luke cosseting anyone, especially a house surgeon, was even harder to believe. 'Sophie, I just don't believe it!'

'Well, he didn't put it quite like that, miss,' Sophie admitted, 'but that's what he meant. Said you've earned a rest.'

'And is he having breakfast in bed?' Jill smiled, for after all Luke had worked far harder than she had done and carried a heavier load of responsibility.

Sophie laughed at the idea and said that men were no good at balancing trays on their knees. 'He's had his breakfast and gone out. He's full of energy, Mr Haddon.'

Energetic and exhausting. You would have thought even Luke would have welcomed an extra hour or two in bed after the last few days! Perhaps he had gone off to meet the blonde in the photograph. Several times Jill had nearly asked Peter who the girl was, but she hadn't wanted to appear too inquisitive. The hospital grapevine was quite definite that Luke wasn't interested in anyone at Q.C.H., but such an attractive man must have a girl-friend somewhere. Or girl-friends, for the competition was likely to be fierce. Luke was a very eligible bachelor indeed. He would undoubtedly pick and choose.

Jill poured a second cup of tea, lay back against her pillows and wondered what she was going to do with her day. The sky was a uniform grey and rain spattered against the windows. Christmas shopping, of course! Today was December the first, and she might not have another long break for a couple of weeks.

Three hours later, her gay carrier bag stuffed with presents for female relatives and friends, she ended up in a bookshop. She had left her father's present until last, because it was the one on which she lavished most thought. It was as if she compensated for the trickiness of their relationship by the loving care with which she selected his presents. She couldn't go home for Christmas, for she would be expected to spend it in hospital, but she might manage the following weekend. Occasional visits were necessary, if only to maintain the fiction that they were a loving and united family.

Jill pulled out several historical biographies and put them back again. None seemed quite right. She sighed and wrinkled her forehead, wondering whether to give up for today, for she was tired and hungry, and the later she left lunch the more crowded everywhere would be.

'Having problems?' asked a familiar voice, and she swung round, almost into the arms of Luke.

The bay she was in was narrow and bounded by high bookshelves, and Luke's tall figure blocked the exit. Unaccountably Jill's heart started to thump and she felt curiously breathless. He wore an olive-green sweater under a sheepskin jacket, and his dark hair was more ruffled than usual. She noticed these things about him, as if concentrating on externals would minimise her reaction to their unexpected meeting.

'I'm doing my Christmas shopping,' she said in a bright unnatural voice, 'but I don't seem able to find anything for my father.'

Luke asked what type of book she was after, and

when she explained he said there was a new biography of the Duke of Wellington, that had been well reviewed. It was downstairs at the front of the shop. Why not come and look at it? So while he paid for the pile of books under his arm Jill flipped through the one on Wellington and decided to buy it. He came to join her and she thanked him politely for his help. She expected him to leave the shop, but he waited while she went to the counter and held the door open for her when she left. They emerged on to the crowded pavement.

Jill looked up at Luke a little uncertainly. 'Well ... thank you. I'll be off now.'

'Where to?' The wind blew his hair into his eyes and he brushed it back, a smile tugging at the corners of his mouth as if he knew the effect he was having on her.

'Oh, just for some lunch. Goodbye, then,' but he walked along beside her, hands in his pockets, towards Piccadilly Circus.

'Are you meeting someone?'

She nearly said yes, just to get rid of him, but she wasn't a girl who liked telling lies, even the small social ones. 'No, I'm not.'

They had reached a pedestrian crossing, and Luke took her arm as they walked. 'Good,' he said pleasantly, 'then we can have lunch together. I know a little place near here that doesn't get too crowded.'

'I don't think——'

'Come on!' He hustled her across the road, held on to her arm and piloted her along the crowded pavement.

'You don't have to be polite,' she protested.

The grip on her arm tightened. They went over another pedestrian crossing. 'I am not,' Luke said slowly, 'being polite. Don't you think it's time we got to know each other a bit better?'

Jill pulled the collar of her coat up under her chin and gave him a quick look. 'I should have thought we knew each other pretty well by now. We seem to have spent a lot of time together in the last week. Day *and* night!'

They had reached the entrance to a small Italian restaurant. Luke paused with his hand on the door. 'We have, haven't we? That's why hospital romances blossom so quickly!' He stood aside, and startled by his last remark, she walked in ahead of him. It was one of those places where the customers are shut off by compartments: it was the bookshop all over again. Luke slid into the seat opposite her, and Jill's whole body went rigid.

'And they wilt just as fast. Hospital romances,' he added at her puzzled look. 'I steer clear of them myself.'

So he hadn't meant what for one crazy and heart-jolting moment she had thought he meant. Mercifully the proprietor came up with a menu card, and in the business of deciding what they were going to eat she had a brief respite. By the time the man left them her pulse rate was back to normal, but her hand lying on the table was tightly clenched.

Luke covered it with his own. 'Relax, my dear girl. I'm sorry if I upset you. Did I upset you?' He took his hand away, stared intently at her. 'Yes, I can see I have. I shouldn't have put it quite so bluntly. But what I said is true, Jill.' When she remained silent he added quietly, 'We lead an unnatural sort of life in hospital, don't we? Everything seems more dramatic, more intense. Including love affairs.'

'I don't know why you're giving me this lecture,' she said. 'I really don't need it.'

'Don't you, Jill? So you're quite sure about Peter?'

A waiter came with two plates of ravioli, and she spooned cheese on to her portion and avoided Luke's eyes. 'I've told you,' she said carefully, 'that I am not in love with your brother, so I don't need any warnings.'

'But you sit on his bed and kiss him.'

'He kissed me. Oh, honestly, this is a ridiculous conversation!'

'Point taken,' Luke said lightly, 'but you may find it more difficult to convince Peter,' and after that he turned the conversation into less personal channels. By mutual consent they avoided shop. They discussed theatre and music and films, found they had similar tastes, were rather surprised, and laughed over their surprise, drank coffee and left.

On the pavement outside Luke took her parcels as well as his own. 'Shall we get back to Queen's? There's a bus stop just round the corner.'

The bus was crowded, so that passengers stood in the gangway. Overhung by a very fat man, Luke shifted along the seat towards Jill. Their closeness didn't affect him as it did her; she could tell that from his expression. He stared past her at the brightly lit shops already decorated for Christmas, made desultory conversation or fell silent. When they reached the residency he handed over her parcels as they climbed the steps.

In the entrance hall a tall blonde girl was talking to two young doctors. She turned as the front door opened and hurried towards them.

'I was early, Luke. I misjudged the time.'

She wore a fur coat, tightly belted to show off a superb figure, and narrow elegant boots. She looked expensive and very sure of herself. Her accent was American, and she was the girl in the photograph—the one on Luke's desk. Her skin was a shade or two darker than her hair, which was explained when Luke asked what time she'd left Los Angeles. Californians were tanned even in winter. Beside her vibrant good health Jill felt pallid and uninteresting, with her Lon-

don complexion made paler by late nights and lack of
fresh air.

The girl was reaching up to kiss Luke on the cheek.
He held her hands for a moment while he smiled at
her with obvious approval, and told her she looked
wonderful. Jill would have faded quietly away, but
Luke insisted on introducing the two girls. 'This is Dr
Bentley, Karen. We work together. Karen and her
family were very kind to me, Jill, when I was in California.'

Karen's smile didn't quite reach her eyes; her look
was assessing and very thorough. Then she tucked a
proprietorial hand through Luke's arm. 'I am just
dying for a cup of your English tea,' she stated. 'I came
straight round here as soon as I'd unpacked.'

'I'm flattered,' Luke said easily, and they went off
down the corridor, arm in arm, a striking and self-
confident pair. The two housemen who had been keeping Karen company while she waited whistled under
their breath.

'Now I know why Haddon shows no interest in the
local talent,' observed one, while the other grinned at
Jill and said jokingly, 'Bad luck, Jill. The competition's tougher than you expected!'

It was one of those silly remarks which mean nothing. Jill dismissed it with a smile, but the smile faded
as she turned the corner. She was a prey to conflicting
emotions, envy of the other girl's poise and beauty,
and an unhappy feeling that she was getting into deep
waters where Luke was concerned. How could you be
attracted to a man you didn't even like? Though after
that last week, when they had spent perhaps fourteen
hours out of every twenty-four in each other's company, it was inevitable that they should have become
closer. Surgery was teamwork, and you needed to respect the leader of your team.

Yes, she did respect Luke, and sometimes she liked

him, and today she had been bowled over by his physical appeal. She undid her parcels to have another look at them, and while she put them away she told herself that she must watch it. She was not going to join the growing band of females at Q.C.H. who drooled over Luke Haddon.

Rumours about Luke's American girl-friend spread around the hospital with astonishing speed. Next morning in Theatre, when they were alone for a few minutes in the changing room, Jan Wyman asked Jill if it was true. 'They say her father's an oil millionaire,' Jan added wistfully, and Jill agreed that she might well be, if the girl's clothes were anything to go by.

In fact he was a peach king, Peter told her. 'You know—Californian tinned peaches. Big and golden and juicy—rather like Karen.' He was pleased with this simile and chose to elaborate it. 'Showy, but lacking in flavour. I prefer the smaller ones with more quality.' He kissed the tip of Jill's nose, then her mouth with more passion. They were alone in his room. Registrars rated two rooms, a bedroom and a sitting room, but it was not like the R.S.O.'s, a self-contained flat. Jill extricated herself from his arms.

'I came to talk about that patient on Lister.' But she couldn't resist adding, 'When did you meet her?'

'Last night, before he took her out on the town. She's over with Daddy, and staying predictably at the Hyde Park Hilton.' His tone was disparaging, which surprised Jill, for Karen was just the sort of girl he usually admired. Perhaps it was a mild case of sour grapes! Though Peter had never seemed jealous of the talented and successful Luke.

'Do you think they're planning to get married?'

Peter shrugged. 'Who knows? Luke's a close devil. But she must be pretty keen on him to follow him over so soon.'

That thought was a curiously depressing one. Jill

left, rather hastily, because Peter showed signs of getting out of hand again. She worried over this problem, because she was a kind girl and didn't like hurting his feelings. The trouble was that in the beginning, when she was raw and inexperienced on the surgical firm, she had welcomed his attentions. Welcomed his friendliness at least; only Peter had misinterpreted the reason. He was not conceited, but he had always been popular with women and he wasn't used to being rebuffed. She had a moment's pang while she wished quite intensely that it was Luke who was interested in her, and not his brother. Then she dismissed the thought firmly, for that way lay nothing but unhappiness.

Luke steered clear of emotional entanglements with his colleagues. He had said so only yesterday. He had a rich and beautiful girl-friend. And anyhow, even if he liked Jill a little, which was doubtful, he thought of her as his brother's girl—that in itself was sufficient reason for him not to get involved with her.

CHAPTER FIVE

CHRISTMAS in a great teaching hospital was an experience that Jill would remember all her life. For weeks beforehand staff and students, and even some of the long-term patients, prepared for it. This year money was tight, and the hospital secretary had made severe cuts in his usually generous financial contributions.

The Christmas committee, with commendable determination, set about raising their own funds, and improvised when money ran short. Old decorations were turned out and refurbished. Cotton wool and plaster of Paris came in very handy for snow scenes, the fitter patients were given coloured crêpe paper bought in bulk, and told to use their imagination. Mrs Christie, who had been a seamstress before she retired, turned out to be more talented than most, and bullied or cajoled the other women patients when they showed signs of flagging.

'Jenner's going to be the prettiest ward in the hospital,' she stated, 'so get on with it, girls. I need three more Santas for the window ledges.'

Jill, perched precariously on a chair while she fixed a robin redbreast to the wall, felt obliged to demur. 'The children's ward is even better.'

'Well, of course, love.' Mrs Christie never called the house surgeons doctor! 'That goes without saying. We expect the kiddies to have the best.' Mrs Christie looked down the ward to where the Haddon brothers had just entered. Peter was worried about an old woman he had operated on the day before, and had asked Luke to come and see her. Concentrating on her task, Jill was unaware of them until Peter ran a finger down the back of her leg.

'Not bad,' he said. 'They'd have looked better in a mini, though.'

She turned quickly, then jumped lightly from the chair. 'What do you think of it?' she asked, gesturing at the decorations.

'Corny but colourful,' Peter grinned, but Luke stalked by with the briefest of glances.

'You are on duty, Miss Bentley? Then don't get too carried away by the Chrismas spirit.'

As Jill followed them down to the far end of the ward where old Mrs Mason lay behind drawn curtains, Mrs Christie gave her the thumbs-up sign. 'Don't mind him, dearie! His bark's definitely worse than his bite.'

Whether she intended him to or not, Luke's sharp ears picked up this remark. He stuck his head out from the curtains and told Jill to step on it, because he was waiting to hear how Mrs Mason's fluid balance was doing. And he added rather grimly that he had been known to bite.

Jill slipped through the curtains and stood beside him, eyes on the old lady's shrunken face. It was terribly sad to be ill at Christmas, especially when she had a large and jolly family, who looked after her with loving care. Far more poignant, however, were the people who chose to have their operations in the pre-Christmas weeks, because otherwise they would have spent the holiday alone.

Jill gave the information that Luke wanted and listened soberly while he discussed the old lady's condition. Peter favoured operating again, because he suspected internal haemorrhage, but Luke, with his greater experience, advised against it.

'Would you mind writing something down?' Peter spread the case notes in front of his brother. He was covering himself, quite understandably, because he was not entirely convinced by Luke's argument. If things went wrong, Luke as the senior man would carry the responsibility. Luke smiled faintly and scribbled a few words. His clinical notes were always brief and to the point. Jill leant forward to read them, and as he straightened Luke quirked an eyebrow at her.

'Well, Miss Bentley, who do you think's right?'

'I'm ... not sure.' She must learn not to behave like an idiot girl when he spoke to her. 'You, probably.'

'She's only trying to flatter you,' Peter joked as they walked back down the ward, but Luke, looking preoccupied, paid no attention. He told Sister about the new treatment he wanted for the old lady, and left them, still looking abstracted, for when Luke's thoughts were on a surgical problem he had no time for anything else.

Next day, which was Christmas Eve, they decorated the residency. The long common-room was festooned with streamers, the old-fashioned paintings of London street scenes were besprigged with holly, and Peter climbed on to Bill Mackie's sturdy shoulders to fix some mistletoe over the doorway. When Jill came in before supper he swooped on her and kissed her soundly, to a background chorus of whistles and comments. Jill, who was shy, pushed him away.

'Don't take him too seriously,' Gwyneth advised. 'He's just practising for tomorrow's party.' Peter returned her sharp smile, but refrained from an equally sharp retort.

'That reminds me, everybody, I think we should have a last practice for the show.' The residents traditionally gave a Christmas show, a half hour of short sketches, songs and music. They toured the wards with it, omitting only those where the patients were too ill to enjoy it. Jill had a very minor part in one of the sketches as a residency maid. The jokes related to hospital life, and Sir James, who had seen it all before more times than he cared to remember, had been heard to say that this year he was not going to stay after midday.

On Christmas Day the surgeons carved the turkeys on the wards. Jill, who had been up for hours because they were still worried about old Mrs Mason, would have liked a rest but felt obliged to help. Not all the ward orderlies had come in, and Sister was delighted to have another pair of hands to carry the dinner trays. Sir James, in a chef's cap and a voluminous white apron, sliced the bird expertly, the while he kept up a running commentary on past Christmases. 'Not what they used to be, my dear, though they say the Christmas show is quite amusing. Perhaps I shall watch it after all. Your young man's the producer, isn't he?'

'My ... Peter isn't ... well, yes, he is the producer,' Jill stammered rather confusedly, because she was put out to discover that even Sir James was linking her name with Peter's.

'What she means,' a cool voice explained from over her shoulder, 'is that she's taking time to make up her mind.'

Jill blushed, and Sir James twinkled benignly. A couple of sherries with Sister, before he started to carve, had put him in a good mood. 'Her feminine prerogative,' he suggested.

Luke didn't return his smile. 'But hard on my brother? Could you spare two minutes, sir, to discuss Mrs Mason?'

Sir James sighed heavily, but he was carving his last plateful, and work must come before pleasure. 'Certainly, my boy. Certainly.' He laid a hand on Luke's shoulder and they went out of the ward together while Sister gave Jill the last two meals.

The residents didn't have a set lunch on Christmas Day. They filled up with savouries and nuts and fruit on the wards, and drank a good deal if they were off duty, abstemiously if they were on. At three o'clock the

Christmas show began in Jenner Ward. Jill watched the other acts, some of which she hadn't seen before, laughed heartily at the skit on Out-patients, applauded Gwyneth's sweet clear soprano doing full justice to an old Welsh song, and made quick preparations for her own appearance. She pinned on the saucy little cap, slipped the frilly pink apron over her own dress, and was metamorphosed into a pretty and flirtatious maid.

'You look exactly like Milly,' Peter grinned. 'Pity you don't behave like her.'

Milly was the youngest and flightiest of the residency maids, and the personnel officer had been heard to say that if she didn't mend her ways she would be transferred to the Sisters' Home. 'Turn round,' Peter ordered, and busied himself in tying a neat bow at her waist. He spun her round again to face him. 'You look very sweet, doesn't she, Luke?'

Luke, leaning against the wall, clarinet in one hand, looked her up and down. 'Very fetching,' he drawled.

'On you go.' Peter gave her a little push and she slipped through the ward doors with the other three actors in the sketch. They were well received and the applause was more than polite, though the jokes were far from original and the acting fairly amateurish. But it was Christmas Day, and the patients and their relatives appreciated the effort that these hard-working young men and women had put into their performance. With Peter in charge the show ran smoothly, with none of those long intervals that are the bane of most amateur productions.

As Jill and her friends came out of the ward Luke walked in, and within seconds a short piece by Mozart sounded on the air. Jill was astonished; he played like a professional. He followed Mozart with a carol, and lastly a sweet and sentimental song which brought a storm of applause. They begged him to play again, and smiling he obliged, but shook his head when they asked for more. 'Sorry, everybody, I've work to do.'

As his tall figure disappeared through the swing
doors at the end of the ward, Jill stared after him. 'I
had no idea he could play like that!'

'Yes, he's almost a virtuoso,' Peter agreed. 'My
brother Luke is a very talented chap. Come on, love,
we all sing now.' They launched into the finale of
their show, and those of the patients who felt like it
joined in. Jill sang as loudly as anyone, but while she
sang her thoughts were with the gifted and quirky
Luke.

The residents ate their Christmas dinner that evening, and anyone who wished was allowed to invite one
guest—wives, girl-friends, relatives, though a fair number of them, like Jill, came on their own. It didn't
matter because they all knew each other. On this occasion there was no formality and everyone sat where
they pleased. The R.S.O. and the surgical registrars
were predictably elected to do the carving. The maids
handed round the first course and then disappeared,
leaving the Christmas puddings and mince pies on hot
plates. Jill sat between Peter and Bill. She had half
expected him to invite one of his favourite nurses, but
when she said this he gave her a look of mock reproach
and addressed himself to Bill.

'This girl still hasn't got the message. She thinks I'm
not serious. What do I do to convince her?'

'Stop eyeing that redhead on Lister,' Bill suggested
drily, and Jill began to laugh. Peter might think himself seriously interested in her, but it was true that he
still had a roving eye. He liked pretty girls, and would
never be faithful to one for any length of time. It was
one of the reasons why she was glad that she hadn't got
seriously involved. One of the reasons. Another was
Luke, and her ambivalent feelings towards him. She
glanced up the table to where he sat, an empty place
on his right.

'Is someone missing?'

'Karen,' said Peter, and at that moment Karen Coleman walked in, only walked was not the right word. Karen made an entrance, a beautiful blonde with a swinging walk and a ready smile.

'Sorry I'm late, honey, but Pop had some friends in for drinks and I was acting hostess.'

And very well she must have done it, Jill thought, envying the other girl's poise and assurance. She wondered about the protracted stay that Karen and her father were making, and when she asked Peter he explained that Mr Coleman was setting up a factory near London. 'And Karen is setting up Luke!' he ended cynically. 'She aims to have a ring on her finger before the New Year!'

'Don't you like her?' Jill asked, for his tone had been critical.

Peter shrugged. 'She's so obvious. Oh, she's dishy all right, but too sure of herself.'

'Luke is obviously charmed.' Had she said that too sharply? With envy? Or with regret?

Peter wasn't one to notice undertones. 'Is she?' he asked carelessly. 'Hard to tell with old Luke. He was never one to show his feelings.'

'He's pleased she's come.' Why did she have to go on about it? But somehow it was difficult to stop.

Peter looked towards his brother and the American girl, 'Well, she is very decorative. She brightens the place up, doesn't she?'

'Like the fairy on the Christmas tree,' Bill said drily, and in her glittery top, with diamond ear pendants that swung and sparkled as she turned her head, Karen did look artificial. She turned her head a great deal, for the residents were plainly fascinated and competed eagerly for her attention.

Karen quite obviously adored being the centre of attraction, while Luke sat, smiling faintly and turning the one glass of wine he had allowed himself round and round. He looked abstracted, remote, and Jill wondered how a jolly extrovert like the American girl could be in love with him. For there seemed little doubt that she was in love. She drew her chair closer to Luke's, slid a hand through his arm and smiled up into his face. 'Luke honey,' she urged, 'surely you could drink a little more wine?' but Luke shook his head.

'No, Karen, I'm on duty. You have another glass.'

Jill was not on call for emergency admissions, but she was looking after all the patients on Sir James' firm, for Bill was off duty. So she too was abstemious and later, when they started dancing in the common-room, she slipped away to do her night round. A young woman on Jenner Ward, who had been under observation for some days, was complaining of pain. Jill was worried about her and tried to contact Peter, but she couldn't find him. The man on switchboard, sounding fed up, said that Mr Haddon was a right one for forgetting his bleep!

'Do you want me to ring round the wards, doctor?'

'Don't bother, it would only disturb the patients.' She decided to consult the R.S.O., but when she got back to the common-room to find the party well away, someone said that Luke had gone up to his flat. Conversation on the telephone would be impossible in this noise, Jill thought. Quicker to go and talk to Luke directly.

When she knocked on his door it was opened by Karen, and Jill wondered if she had been tactless in coming. The girl was in her stockinged feet, but even so she topped Jill by several inches. The smooth glowing face smiled down at her. Jill stared, fascinated, at her perfect white teeth. 'Hi, honey. What can I do for you?'

Jill looked past her into the empty room. 'I wanted

some advice. Do you know where Luke is?'

Karen shook her head, and the earrings bobbed up and down. She glided back to the sofa and sank on to it, piling the cushions comfortably behind her head. 'Sorry, but stop and talk to me. He said he'd be back soon.'

So Jill shut the door and joined Karen by the old-fashioned coal fire, and the American girl became quite expansive. 'You're Peter's girl, aren't you? Luke introduced us that time in the hall.'

'I work with Peter,' Jill said cautiously, and Karen giggled.

'Shall I make a confession? When you came in with Luke that day I could have scratched your eyes out.' She smiled widely as she said this, so presumably she no longer regarded Jill as a potential rival. It was impossible not to like her. She radiated health and wellbeing, and a kind of bouncy good nature that was very endearing.

Jill smiled back at her. 'Honestly, if I looked like you I wouldn't be worrying about other girls.' There was a trace of wistfulness in her voice which the young American must have spotted, for she swung her nylon-clad feet down and leant forward.

'You're quite something yourself, honey, with that black hair and that marvellous skin. If you weren't Peter's girl I'd still consider you a threat, believe you me!'

'But I'm not—oh, what's the use!' Jill gave up in exasperation. Useless to keep repeating the same old thing.

Karen looked knowing. 'Luke says you're playing hard to get. Good tactics, I guess, with a man like Peter.'

Jill coloured with anger. 'He had no right to say that! It's not true.'

Karen lay back on the sofa again and put her hands

behind her head. 'Don't be offended, it shows you're real smart. But I'll tell you something. It wouldn't work on Luke!'

Annoyed though she was, Jill had to smile. Karen was shrewder than she appeared. When Luke returned he looked surprised to see her, but he accompanied her most willingly to the ward, and agreed that she had been right to call him.

'Her ulcer has perforated. Lay on theatre and the anaesthetist, will you?' He glanced at his watch. 'Any time after eleven.'

'Will you want me to assist?' Jill asked.

She wasn't on for emergencies, but this was her patient. Luke was scribbling a few words in the case notes. He shrugged and went on writing. 'It's up to you. I don't mind as long as someone does.'

The indifference with which he said this stung. 'Then if it's up to me I won't,' Jill snapped. 'There are two house surgeons on call. Get one of them.'

Luke looked astonished at this outburst. He scrawled an illegible signature at the bottom of his notes, and pushed back his chair. 'What was that about?' he asked softly. They were alone in Sister's office and the door was shut. Jill put out a hand to slide it back, cursing herself for that childish loss of temper. It had been Luke's remark to Karen that had really rankled, only she would have died rather than admit it.

Luke was across the small room in two strides and his hand came down on hers, pushing the door shut again. 'I asked you a question, Jill.' He took his hand off hers and put it under her chin, tilting her head up and staring down at her. 'That was rude and un-necessary, and I want to know why.'

'Let me go,' she whispered, and then because she wanted only to get away from him, 'All right, I'm sorry. I expect I'm tired.'

The dark eyes held hers. 'You don't look tired. In

fact you're looking remarkably fresh and pretty. So as a punishment for that display of petulance you can assist me with Mrs Brown.'

'You said you didn't mind who went to theatre.'

'I've changed my mind. Let me know if eleven suits everyone else. I'll be in my flat,' and he rolled the door back and stepped through.

Jill's heart was thumping as she sat down at the desk and began to telephone. She had been an idiot to tangle with Luke—he would always get the best of it. When she had fixed up theatre and the anaesthetist she was tempted to ask one of the house surgeons on call to assist, but she hadn't quite got the courage. Luke was more than capable of sending for her if she didn't turn up. Whether he really had the authority to demand her presence in theatre was another matter, but she didn't want to put it to the test. House surgeons were easy to come by, the competition for jobs was fierce, and acquiring a reputation for being difficult didn't help when one applied for one's next post.

In theatre Luke virtually ignored her, though he chatted away to the anaesthetist, and was charming to Jan Wyman. When Jan asked him afterwards if he would like a cup of tea, he thanked her nicely but said he must be off. Jan looked disappointed and the anaesthetist grinned.

'Back to his popsie! And I don't blame him. She's quite an armful!'

Jan glanced up at the clock. 'Surely she'll have gone? It's after twelve.'

'Not on your life,' said the anaesthetist. 'We left her in the common-room, chatting up the lads.'

She was not in the common-room when Jill called in there on her way to bed. Nor was Luke. Jill accepted a small drink as a nightcap and tried to join in the fun, but she kept thinking of Karen, stretched out on the sofa in Luke's flat, looking very much at home and extremely pleased with herself. Were they together now, making love, and would Luke ask her to marry him? Jill wrenched her thoughts away from these unhappy speculations, and told herself fiercely that she hated Luke. What she felt for him was based entirely on physical attraction. She couldn't love a man who was a tyrant and a bully.

Then Peter came back from his night rounds and persuaded her to dance, and because she wanted to prove to herself how little Luke meant, she was more forthcoming than usual to him, a fact on which he was quick to comment.

'You act as if you're pleased to see me. Are you?' He held her closer and rubbed his cheek against hers.

'I'm always pleased to see you,' Jill smiled, and that was true, because Peter was friendly and uncomplicated. He would never speak to one of his house surgeons as Luke had spoken to her.

'I wish you were off duty entirely,' he murmured, lips close to her ear. 'I wish there was a bit more privacy in this damn place.'

'Well, there isn't,' Jill said, and was thankful for it. She didn't want Peter coming to her room later, and she didn't want a scene when she told him to go away. If only, she thought sadly, she had fallen in love with Peter instead of Luke, how much simpler things would have been! She disengaged herself from Peter's arms, 'I really am tired. I think I'll go to bed.'

The lift was stuck on another floor, so she dragged wearily upstairs, and while she undressed the thoughts tumbled around in her mind. She did love Luke! She had admitted it to herself. No, she didn't love him. But how she envied Karen! He had touched her hand tonight, and held her chin in hard fingers. She had wanted quite desperately to throw her arms around him and cling to him, but his reaction had been entirely one of disapproval and displeasure. He had looked at her coldly and issued his orders. She was a house surgeon and he was R.S.O., and he would never see her in any other way, except as the girl who played hard to get with his brother.

And that was just one more nail in her coffin as far as he was concerned.

CHAPTER SIX

JILL had telephoned her family on Christmas Eve and arranged to go home the following weekend. She never did this with much enthusiasm, so when it started to snow on the Friday morning she kept glancing out of the ward windows, hoping that they were in for a heavy fall. If the rail services were disrupted she would have a good excuse to stay in London.

By Friday evening snow blanketed the streets and the weather man predicted more to follow. She had intended catching the night train, but now she could cancel her visit with a clear conscience. She would let her father know she wasn't coming as soon as she had finished one or two jobs on the wards. At six o'clock, however, Sister came out of her office to say that she was wanted on the telephone.

'Long distance, Dr Bentley.'

Her father, with the harassed manner that seemed second nature to him nowadays, urged her to cancel her visit.

'I'd already decided to, Dad. I'll come when the weather improves.'

'Perhaps you'll see us in London before then. Your mother and Betty are very keen to go up for a few days.'

Jill still hated it when he called Marcia Bentley her mother. Her fingers tightened round the telephone receiver. With any luck they might pick one of her weekends on duty. 'When, Dad?'

'Depends on the weather, and when I'm free. I must ring off, Jill. I'm in the middle of a surgery.'

Dr Bentley was the senior partner in a two-man practice and worked very hard. Jill had suffered many a pang when she looked at his lined careworn face.

The practice was a heavy responsibility, and his home life was by no means restful—at least it hadn't been as long as Jill was there. However hard they all tried, there was tension and an undercurrent of hostility between the three women. He had sounded genuinely sorry that she wasn't coming home, but Jill was relieved. She would go to bed early, treat herself to a lie-in the following morning.

In fact she arrived in the dining-room for mid-morning coffee, having missed breakfast altogether. Gwyneth greeted her with surprise.

'I thought you were going home.'

Jill gestured at the windows, half obliterated by snow. 'In this? Wouldn't have been worth it.'

'Pleased to have an excuse?' Gwyneth knew all about her family problems.

Jill nodded, poured coffee and sat beside her friend. Luke stared at her from across the big table. 'That sounds bad. Why do you need an excuse?'

'Because she hates her family.' Hate was too strong a word, but Gwyneth always exaggerated.

'Gwyneth, that's not true!'

'You've told me often enough how awful your step-mother is.'

Jill didn't want her family problems dissected publicly, and especially not before Luke. 'Did you hear the weather forecast?' she asked brightly, but Gwyneth was not to be deflected.

She addressed herself to Luke, her lilting Welsh voice indignant. 'Jill has had a rotten time all her life, between her stepmother and her stepsister. They've never shown her anything but antagonism.'

That too was an exaggeration, because Marcia was erratic in her behaviour, swinging between hostility and tentative attempts at reconciliation. Luke's glance slid to Jill's hot face. 'You've met them, Gwyneth?'

'Well, no ... but Jill's told me ...'

His expression became ironical. 'So you've only heard one side. Jill can be prickly herself sometimes.' He leant forward, smiling quizzically. 'Can't you, Jill?'

Since Christmas night Jill had avoided him as much as possible. She thought that he knew this and was amused by it. Once or twice she had caught him looking at her speculatively, on ward rounds or at meals. She made some noncommittal reply and Luke shrugged and departed.

'What is it about you two?' Gwyneth asked, her thin clever face thoughtful.

Jill tensed, afraid that Gwyneth might guess her secret. The Welsh girl was her friend, but a great one for gossip. 'We just can't seem to hit it off,' she said casually. 'Are you still one of his admirers?'

'Of course I am. He's got brains and personality——'

'Oh, for goodness' sake, Gwyneth,' one of the housemen interposed, 'we all know how wonderful Luke Haddon is. Personally I can't stand the chap.'

That was how people seemed to feel about Luke; they either loved him or hated him. A good deal of the dislike, Jill thought, was motivated by envy, because he was going straight to the top. His detractors said he had an unfair advantage because of his connections, though they admitted that he would have got there anyway. The only difference was that it might have taken a little longer.

She was still lingering over her coffee when Peter came in and sat down beside her. 'Luke told me you'd cancelled your trip. He wants us to make up a foursome tonight, go out for a meal.'

'A ... foursome?'

'Karen and him, you and me. How about it?'

Jill was surprised, both that Luke should suggest it and Peter should agree. Since Christmas she had kept him at a distance, because she was an honest girl and it would have been the height of dishonesty to go out with Peter when she was attracted to his brother. Even if what she felt for Luke turned out to be nothing more than a temporary infatuation, she would never love a man like Peter. He had many good qualities, but he wasn't for her.

So she hesitated, and Peter looked rueful. 'You can't pretend you have anything on.' The table had emptied and there was no one near them. 'You've changed lately, Jill. Any reason?'

She gazed at him unhappily. 'Oh, Peter ... it's not easy to explain.'

'Try,' he suggested, putting his head close to hers. If it had been Luke her heart would have thumped in her chest. The mystery of physical attraction was hard to explain, for Peter was in the conventional sense better-looking than his brother. She moistened her lips nervously. 'Peter, people are looking at us.'

'Oh, to hell with other people,' he said under his breath. 'They know how I feel about you.'

'How do you feel?'

'What is this, Jill? You know quite well.'

'No, I don't,' Jill said worriedly, 'I think it's just a passing fancy. I hope so, Peter, because I like you very much, but that's all.'

His smile became a little strained, and he drew back and turned his attention to his coffee. The residents at the other end of the table were leaving. Peter stirred vigorously and waited for them to go. 'Pity. You used to give a different impression.'

Had she? She had enjoyed his company, been flattered by his attentions, but never surely pretended more than she had felt. When she said so Peter shrugged moodily. 'All right, Jill, I suppose I read more into the situation than was there. Funny, it's usually the girl who does that.' He drained his cup and poured more. 'So that's why you've given me the warning light lately? I thought it was just a stage in the game.'

That sentence made Jill feel better. If he looked on his relationships with women as a game, then he couldn't be serious. He couldn't be hurt. He would transfer his affections to another girl and lose all interest in her. 'I have to go,' she said quickly, 'I'm meeting Jan Wyman.'

'We haven't arranged anything about tonight.'

Surprised, she could only stare. Peter smiled up at her, outwardly back to normal. 'You are coming?'

'But why, Peter? After what I've just said?'

'Why not? You did say you liked me still. Or is it because Luke will be there?'

If Peter knew where they stood she could accept with a clear conscience. If she wanted to go. 'All right,' she said a little hesitantly, and making a joke of it, 'You'll have to protect me from Luke.'

'Are you that frightened of him? Seven-thirty, then. Meet you in the main hall.'

When she told Jan where she was going that evening the other girl was frankly envious. They were sitting in the underground, travelling out to Jan's home in Golders Green. 'Is it true what the residents say? That Luke's madly in love with that American girl?'

'I suppose he must be. She really is beautiful ... and nice too.'

Jan looked out of the window as they rattled into a station. 'It's silly, eating your heart out for someone who hardly notices your existence. Isn't it?' she ended fiercely.

There was no one opposite them. Jill squeezed the other girl's hand. 'He admires you, Jan. He thinks you're a splendid theatre Sister.'

Jan gave a laugh that ended in a sob. 'And that's a great comfort! But it *is* silly, when there are plenty of other men around. That new anaesthetic registrar, for instance. And I can hardly bother to talk to him.'

'You should bother,' Jill said. 'He's nice, and he likes

you very much.' She added rather sadly, 'He's probably much nicer than Luke,' and then the train drew into their station and the conversation ended.

It was the first time Jill had visited Jan's home. She spent a happy day with the Wymans and would have liked to stay on to supper with them, for she was beginning to regret that she had accepted Peter's invitation. It had been weak and foolish, giving way to the urge to spend a few hours in Luke's company. It could only make her unhappy, seeing him with Karen.

When she went down to the hall of the residency Peter was waiting for her. He smiled his approval of her appearance and told her the others were meeting them in the hospital car park. They were using Luke's car, and Karen sat beside him in the front seat.

'Hi, honey. Isn't this fun!' Karen bubbled enthusiastically. 'We're going to that new place in Chelsea.'

With Karen in the car no one else needed to do much talking. Jill stared at the back of Luke's head, and wondered if he ever got tired of the American girl's exuberance. Certainly he was saying very little in return. The restaurant was crowded, but Luke had booked a table. The girls went to the ladies' room, and while Karen fussed with an already perfect hair-do, she beamed into the mirror at Jill.

'I just love that dress of yours.'

She would probably have said the same thing whatever Jill was wearing. Karen was not insincere, but she liked to please. Everyone. Men *and* women. Doubtless she was very good at pleasing Luke.

Jill didn't bother to do anything to her appearance; she had after all spent a considerable time on it quite recently. She stared at her reflection critically. Dark hair, pale face, slender figure in a blue-green ankle-length dress. She wasn't bad-looking, but she lacked Karen's lush and extravagant beauty. She couldn't compete, and it was a waste of time trying.

Dinner was a leisurely affair. They sat at a table on a wide balcony, while people who were dancing circulated below. When they reached the sweet stage Jill said she couldn't eat a thing more, she would just have coffee, so Peter seized her hand and led her off to the dance floor. As they went down the steps they heard Karen telling Luke that she would just love a slice of that gorgeous-looking gateau.

Jill giggled. 'Where does she put it? And why doesn't she get fat?'

'She takes plenty of exercise. Even in London she swims every day, and plays squash with Luke when he's free.'

'She seems ... such an unlikely friend for Luke.'

'Yes, I know, but she makes him laugh.' Peter steered her on to the dance floor. 'I suppose you might say she's a bit of light relief.'

But was that a good enough basis for marriage? Wasn't it just possible that Luke was simply enjoying Karen's company, her beauty and her undoubted sex appeal? That she would go back to the States in a few weeks' time with no hard feelings on either side? She must have dozens of boy-friends when she looked like that. Jill said a little of this to Peter as they moved slowly round the floor.

'Dunno,' he murmured with marked lack of interest, and brushed her hair with his lips. Later, when he asked her to dance again, she said that her ankle was still playing up, especially in the sandals she was wearing. Luke eyed the flimsy straps disapprovingly.

'What silly shoes women wear! Dance with Karen, Peter. I'm feeling rather tired myself.'

That was an unusual admission from Luke. Jill studied him across the table, noticing for the first time the shadows under his eyes, and the way he kept rubbing his forehead. 'You're not enjoying this, are you?' she asked quietly, and Luke smiled wryly.

'I'd have preferred somewhere quieter, but Karen wanted to come here.' The band was pumping out an exuberant number, and he winced and shut his eyes. 'Sorry to be a wet blanket. Truth is, I've a filthy headache. I get them now and then.'

Jill knew that he had been up till three last night, and the night before he had been out with a party of Americans. 'Not enough sleep,' she murmured, and leant forward to touch his hand gently. 'Luke? I've some aspirins in my bag. Would you like some?'

'Never touch the things.'

She reached for his empty glass, dropped two aspirins in, added water from a carafe, and shook it round until the tablets dissolved. Luke opened his eyes and scowled like a small boy. 'Filthy stuff. Why do you carry it around with you?'

'For the odd emergency, like now. I get headaches too. Come on, drink up.' She smiled at him very sweetly, wanting only to help, because he looked so exhausted and so unlike himself. Just for a few minutes she was at ease with him. They were at ease together. Luke responded to her mood, drinking the mixture, but pulling a face.

'You know this stuff is bad for you? Can cause acute ulcers and haemorrhage in a few people.'

'Yes, doctor, but the risk's not very great if you only take it occasionally.' She touched his hand again. 'Please don't feel you have to talk. Just relax and let it work.'

He rested his cheek on his palm and shut his eyes. Jill looked at his lean, strong-featured face, at the surprisingly long lashes and the firm mouth. I do love him, she thought. It isn't just physical attraction. I would like to look after him and make him live more sensibly—go to bed early when he has the chance, catch up on all that lost sleep. That's what Karen should be doing instead of dragging him out to places like this.

'You're a nice girl, Jill. I owe you an apology.' Luke made the remark without opening his eyes.

'An apology for what?'

He looked at her then, a ghost of a smile tugging at his lips. 'For thinking you weren't a nice girl. For doubting your integrity.'

They stared at one another. A little shyly Jill said that she was glad. Perhaps they could be friends from now on? Friendship was better than nothing. It was all she could expect.

When Karen and Peter came back there was a great deal of laughter and good-natured banter between the two of them. Jill contributed very little to the conversation, and Luke nothing at all, but they didn't seem to notice. They were pleased with each other, enjoying the evening. At ten o'clock Luke sat up straight in his chair, smiled at Jill and asked her to dance.

'I feel fine now,' he assured her. 'Headache's gone.'

They danced well together. Luke was light on his feet and knew how to lead. Jill drifted in his arms, happy and relaxed, wondering why she had been so reluctant to come.

'Did you hear what I said?' His grip on her hand tightened for a moment. 'Karen and Peter are hitting it off very well, aren't they?'

She followed the direction of his eyes. The other two were still at the table, heads close together, talking animatedly. She was struck by the thought that those two were more suited to each other than Karen and Luke. If only Karen would transfer her affections! But even if she did Luke was not likely to look in her direction. Hadn't he told her once that he steered clear of involvement with his women colleagues?

At midnight Luke suggested leaving and Karen

pouted at him prettily. 'It's so early, honey. I could dance all night!'

Was she thoughtless or selfish, or did she understand so little about a surgeon's life that she didn't realise Luke might be tired? He looked better now, but still not himself.

'Luke was up until three last night,' said Jill, and Karen glanced at her with surprise.

'So what? I wasn't in bed much earlier myself.'

'But you didn't have to work next day!' Jill cried, annoyed with the American girl for being so obtuse. 'Can't you see that he's tired?'

Karen's big blue eyes widened, and she subjected Luke to a thorough scrutiny. 'He looks O.K. to me. Are you tired, honey?'

'A little, but we'll stay if you want to. Only don't expect me to dance.' He smiled as he said this, then looked from Karen to Jill. '*You've* got a gammy ankle and *I'm* feeling whacked. Mind sitting it out with me while these two energetic types entertain each other?'

Neither Karen nor Peter seemed to mind this arrangement. They went off quite happily together, and Jill sat watching the dancers, saying very little because she sensed Luke wasn't in the mood for conversation. She was in no way offended by his silence. She was happy just to be with him, to feel that she was giving him the chance to relax a little, to unwind.

When they finally left they dropped Karen off first at her hotel. On the short drive back to the hospital Jill fell asleep with her head against Peter's shoulder. She woke with a start to find Luke holding the car door open, and Peter gently shaking her.

'Come on, sleepyhead. I'll see you up to your room.'

Her last waking thought before she fell into bed was of Luke's dark face smiling down at her, as he waited for her to get out of the car. It had been an indulgent smile, and quite different from the sharp sarcastic smiles he had favoured her with in the past.

A few days later Jill received a letter from her stepmother, saying that they were all coming up to London for a few days. 'It's ages since we were in London,' Marcia wrote, 'but it gets harder every year to prise your father out of his chair.' She was another, like Karen, who had no understanding of the stressful lives most doctors lead. And with less excuse than Karen, Jill thought bitterly, because she had lived with one for the last twenty years.

They were to stay at a small family hotel in Kensington, a comfortable but rather dull establishment, favoured by Dr Bentley and despised by his wife. On the night of their arrival Jill had dinner with them there, and Marcia, looking discontentedly around at the middle-aged to elderly diners, commented that it wouldn't be much fun for Betty. Such a pity they couldn't have found a smarter place!

She was the type of woman who has to grumble about something, and yet in her own way she was a good wife. She was an excellent cook, saw that her husband was always well turned out, and kept herself smart. In short she managed the material side of marriage better than most. Better certainly than Jill's mother, who had had a loving heart but a disorganised mind.

If there was one person Marcia really cared about it was her daughter, of whom she was fiercely protective. Betty sat beside her mother, looking sweet and very feminine. Only those who knew her really well, like Jill, were aware of the calculating mind behind the pretty face. She followed up her mother's last remark by suggesting that she might pay Jill a visit at the hospital tomorrow.

'All those lovely men!' she said with a giggle, and a

flicker of distaste crossed Dr Bentley's face.

'You've been watching too much rubbish on TV, my dear. But if Jill isn't too busy . . .'

Mrs Bentley was meeting a friend tomorrow evening. If Jill took Betty off her father's hands he might have a little time to himself; perhaps meet some old cronies, which he did all too rarely nowadays.

'Come by all means, Betty. I'm on duty, but that doesn't matter. Come about seven and you can have supper with the residents.'

Betty arrived while Jill was doing routine preoperative examinations on four patients for the next day's list. Jill had left her room unlocked and told Betty its number in case she should be held up. When she came back from the wards her room was empty, so she went down to the common-room.

Betty sat by the big stove, a glass of sherry in one hand, looking very young and shy and appealing. Compared to the glamorous Karen her light brown hair and hazel eyes might seem quite ordinary, but no one would have wanted to protect the self-assured American girl. Men were quick to come to Betty's rescue. It happened all the time.

'Hallo, Jill,' said Betty in her soft breathy little voice. 'I met Mr—Mr Haddon when I was wandering around and he brought me down here.' She smiled shyly at Peter and he looked back at her with a faintly puzzled expression. 'I know you said to wait in your room,' Betty rushed on, 'so I hope you don't mind?' Her eyes were anxious, as if she half expected to be told off.

'Of course I don't mind. Thank you for looking after her, Peter.'

'A pleasure,' Peter said gallantly, and Betty dimpled up at him again.

When they went into the dining-room Peter forsook his usual place at the registrars' table and sat between

Jill and her sister. He put himself out to be amusing, telling stories of hospital life that had Betty in paroxysms of giggles. Her round little face was flushed and her eyes were full of tears of laughter, when Luke stopped by them on his way out. He had glanced their way frequently during the meal, and now he smiled down at Betty with obvious curiosity.

'A friend of yours, Jill?'

'My sister,' Jill said, and watched his reaction. Surprise. Disbelief. Amusement. They all flitted across his face, to be replaced by the old sarcastic look he had so often worn when dealing with her in the past.

'Your sister,' he repeated softly, and Jill said quickly, 'This is Mr Haddon, Betty, Peter's brother. The man who keeps us all in order.'

If Betty was impressed by Peter she must be bowled over by Luke! For Betty at eighteen was man-mad, though skilled at concealing it. She held out a small hand, which was engulfed by Luke's, gave him her shy sweet smile, and said it was so nice meeting the people Jill worked with.

'And ... interesting for us to meet Jill's family,' he replied. 'Peter, can you entertain the young lady for a few minutes while I have a word with Jill?'

He had been going round the wards when he noticed that one of Jill's post-operative patients had sprung a temperature. 'I think she has a wound infection. I've put her on ampicillin, but if she doesn't settle we may have to open it.'

They were standing in the corridor outside the dining-room. Betty's gay, bubbling laugh reached their ears and Luke smiled. 'Quite a surprise, your little sister!' he observed.

'Why?' Jill asked, though really she knew.

'Didn't you say you hated her?'

She avoided his eyes, a flush of anger tinging her cheeks. 'No, I didn't. That was what Gwyneth said.'

'But Gwyneth was presumably quoting you?'

'Gwyneth exaggerates. Do you want me to go and see that patient?'

'No need, I've already examined her, but watch out for signs of an abscess.' He shut the dining-room door and eyed her thoughtfully. '*Do* you hate your sister, Jill?'

'Of course I don't hate her!' Jill cried in exasperation. 'I just don't like her very much.' The words once uttered couldn't be retracted. They made her seem mean-spirited, unkind. Luke obviously thought so, for his expression hardened.

'Sounds like a classical case of sibling rivalry,' he commented in his nastiest voice. 'I suppose you never adapted to your father's second marriage.'

'I tried to,' said Jill woodenly, 'but I wasn't given much encouragement.' Why, oh, why had she been stupid enough to say that?

Luke raised his eyebrows in the infuriating way he had. 'You're a big girl now,' he commented unkindly, 'you ought to have got over all that,' and he strode away, leaving her speechless.

Peter did nothing to relieve Jill's ruffled feelings when hours later, after Betty had gone, they met in the kitchen of Jenner Ward over mugs of Ovaltine. 'So that's your ugly sister, Cinderella!' he teased. 'Not quite what I expected.'

Jill took a deep steadying breath. 'I've already been through all that with your brother. He informed me that I'm probably jealous of Betty.' Her voice rose indignantly, and she swallowed and started again. 'I'm not jealous of her, Peter, but I didn't have a very happy childhood, that's for sure.'

Peter hoisted himself on to the kitchen table where she was sitting, and gave her an affectionate hug. 'Don't get so intense about it, Jill dear. But has it ever occurred to you that what Luke said just could be true? How old were you when your father remarried?'

'Nearly five.'

'And you remembered your mother still?'

'Of course I did! Of course!'

Peter studied her thoughtfully. 'So you were old enough to resent a new baby. Not to mention a new mother.'

'I suppose so.'

'And the baby grew into a dear fluffy little girl!'

'Oh, very fluffy,' Jill said drily. 'Grown-ups just adored her! I was a skinny plain little thing with a black ponytail——' She broke off at the expression on Peter's face. 'I wasn't jealous!' she cried passionately. 'I was just telling you how it was.'

Peter's arm was still round her. He dropped a light kiss on her hair. 'All right! All right! Don't get so worked up. But if you could look at the past objectively you might see it in a different light.'

'I want to forget the past. Do stop going on about it.'

'Sorry, my love.' He slid off the table and ambled over to the door. 'But that little dolly's no threat to you, Jill. Surely you can see that?'

Jill sighed and finished her Ovaltine. It was extraordinary how Betty could sow discord in her life, simply by being around. It was bad enough having Luke critical of her attitude to her sister—she had thought that Peter at least would be more understanding. As she walked down the darkened ward, on tiptoe so as not to waken the patients, she thought sadly that it was Luke's reaction which had really hurt. He had just begun to be more friendly, to treat her as if he liked her, and then this evening he had changed back in a couple of minutes to the old sharp-tongued Luke, who looked at her with critical unfriendly eyes.

The night nurse greeted her and while they discussed the patients softly, sitting beside each other at the big table in the centre of the ward, with its shaded light and the case notes handy, Jill forgot her troubles in other people's problems. They came back to plague her, though, when she was in bed. Memory after memory with every detail clear. The time Betty had dropped the brand-new teapot from Jill's birthday tea-set, and screamed when Jill hit her, and sobbed that it had been an accident. They had believed Betty and punished Jill for her loss of temper, for only Jill had seen the smiling malice on her little sister's face as Betty held the teapot high and deliberately dropped it. Scene after scene with the same theme—provocation from Betty, frustration and anger from Jill.

'If you could look at the past objectively you might see it in a different light,' Peter had said. But the past looked just the same from this distance. Betty had been a spiteful little girl, who had grown up into a spiteful young woman. Didn't they say character was formed very early in life? And hadn't Betty had years of practice at concealing her less attractive qualities! Only why, why, thought poor Jill, should it always be herself who came out of every encounter in a bad light? She put her head under the bedclothes, trying to shut out the sounds of doors slamming and the lift shutting, but even when the residency had settled down to relative quiet, it was still a long time before she fell asleep.

CHAPTER SEVEN

Morning brought its usual reaction. Yesterday's events no longer seemed so important. They had been blunted by the passage of hours, and Jill felt a little ashamed that she had allowed the old childhood feelings of resentment and despair to consume her so fiercely. As she dressed for breakfast she wondered uneasily if there might not be at least some truth in Luke's remarks.

Sibling rivalry certainly motivated Betty, and presumably, if she was honest, herself too. And she *was* a big girl now! She should be able to put the past behind her, not let it corrode her present life, the fine, worthwhile happy life that she had built for herself in London. In a few days Betty would be gone. With any luck she might not come round to the residency quarters again. When she met Luke on a ward round, Jill thought how foolish had been the night's heart-searchings. He greeted her in a friendly way, standing beside her in the background, a spectator like herself, rather than an active participant. For this was the Professor of Surgery's teaching round, to which almost everyone went if they were free.

Jill tried hard to concentrate on the Professor's words, but she was intensely conscious of Luke's closeness, and of the two or three occasions when he brushed against her in the crowd. She stole a glance at him once, and was sure that he was totally unaware of the people around him. Luke had enviable powers of concentration, it was one of the chief reasons that he had been such a brilliant student. She was sure that he kept his private life very strictly in its own compartment, for non-working hours. He would never stand on a ward round, as she was doing now, thinking about love and all its problems. That, she thought, was one of the most fundamental differences between men and women.

The Professor rounded off his discussion and moved on to another bed. Luke tapped her on the shoulder and her heart bumped. 'Isn't this the woman Sir James passed over to the surgical unit? Tell me something about her——'

Her thoughts were scattered, difficult to bring together, so Jill stammered, had trouble in giving a concise history. Luke gave her a pitying look and commented that she needed a holiday. Then he softened his remark by the nice smile that only his close friends saw. 'Cheer up, little one. I didn't mean to be unkind.'

If only she could tell him that he always saw her at her worst. That with other people she was efficient, clear-headed, practical. The little episode spoilt the rest of the ward round, and she went back to her room at four o'clock feeling rather depressed. It did nothing to relieve her feelings to find Betty there, lolling on the bed in a pink trouser suit and stockinged feet.

'I thought I locked my door,' said Jill, and Betty waved a dainty hand, tipped with nails the exact colour of her suit.

'The housekeeper lent me her pass-key.' She had, she explained, got tired of shopping, and being in the neighbourhood had thought she would call in. 'A cup of tea would be very welcome.' She widened her eyes and waited for Jill's reaction.

'Would you like it up here?' Silly question! What Betty wanted was to meet the residents again. She said as much quite openly.

'Honestly, Jill, you are lucky. All those super men around. You must have a marvellous time.'

Jill said a little tartly that most of the 'super' men had wives or girl-friends.

'But not all. The Haddon brothers aren't married, and they're the pick of the bunch,' Betty said artlessly.

In spite of herself Jill laughed. 'How do you know?'

'Because I asked, silly. I asked Peter Haddon if his brother was married, and he said no, neither of them were. Will he be there now?'

'Peter?'

'Not Peter. The other one.' Betty's small face became dreamy. 'If only we weren't leaving so soon! I'm sure he liked me.'

'Do grow up,' Jill said impatiently, as they went downstairs. 'Luke has a lovely girl-friend, who's come all the way from America to visit him.'

Betty's smile vanished and she looked sulky, but the sulkiness went when the residents greeted her like an old friend. If she was put out at not seeing Luke she concealed it, and when she left she thanked Jill very prettily for giving her tea. The thanks would have been more perfunctory, Jill knew from experience, if they had been on their own.

The Bentleys planned to leave London on Friday morning, and on Thursday evening Jill went round to their hotel for a farewell meal. She sensed that her father was relieved to be going home, though his womenfolk regretted it. 'The traffic gets worse every year,' he said, 'I don't know how you can bear it, Jill.'

'I'm used to it, Dad, and I love London.'

'You certainly look well on it,' her father agreed. 'Hard work seems to suit you.' He glanced at his younger daughter. 'But it's high time Betty got back to a quiet country life.'

Betty did look out of sorts. She was almost plain tonight, in spite of a lavish hand with the make-up, and she had only toyed with the excellent if unimaginative dinner. The hotel prided itself on serving the best of British food, and Jill for one had thoroughly enjoyed the change from hospital fare.

'You do look tired, Betty,' she commiserated. 'I should have an early night.'

'I'm not tired,' Betty said grumpily, but when Jill rose to go at ten-thirty, she said she might as well go to bed too. There was nothing else to do in this dump! Considering that she had been out every night, Jill thought this singularly ungracious. Even her mother looked annoyed and said sharply that they had deliberately made no plans for this evening, because they would be making such an early start in the morning.

It turned out that they were all up even earlier than expected. At four in the morning the telephone by Jill's bed rang and she fumbled for it in the dark, thinking resentfully that someone had dialled the wrong number, for she was off duty tonight. It wasn't an internal call, however. It was her father, apologising for waking her.

'Betty has appendicitis. She needs admission to hospital.'

It took Jill a few seconds to react. 'You mean here? To Q.C.H.?'

'Where better?' her father asked.

'But, Dad, are you sure?'

'Quite sure. The hotel doctor has just examined her. He's beside me now. Like a word with him?'

'I'd better get this call transferred to Luke Haddon. He accepts new admissions.' She forgot that this was Luke's night off as well, but if he was no better pleased than she had been at being disturbed, he didn't show it. In fact he insisted on operating on Betty himself.

Jill was still dressing when he knocked on her door. She pulled on the trousers that she always wore at night time, and let him in.

'I'm awfully sorry,' she stammered, 'I should have remembered it was your night off.'

He brushed her apology aside. 'Think nothing of it. Only too glad to be of help.'

'Yes, I know, but——'

'Your little sister should be in any minute. The hotel doctor thinks she's already perforated.'

'Surely not so soon?'

Luke hunched his shoulders. 'Silly kid's been sitting on it for a couple of days. Didn't tell your parents she had a tummy-ache. Didn't mention she was sick this morning, nor yesterday morning.'

'Oh, poor Betty! That's why she was so disagreeable this evening!'

'Even worse than usual?' Luke asked with a lift of his eyebrows, and she bit her lip and turned away.

'Do you mind? I have to finish dressing.'

He lounged against the wall and looked her over. 'You're dressed already. Come up to my flat and have a cup of coffee while we wait. I've asked the ward to ring me when she's in.'

'You're going to do her? But Mr Dawson's on call.'

Mr Dawson was the senior surgical registrar, who stood in as R.S.O. on Luke's nights off. 'Certainly I'm going to do her. I suggested the consultant on call, but your father said he'd be quite happy for me to operate. So come on.'

'I'll be up in a minute or two.' Jill felt shy about using the mirror in front of him, but he showed no sign of going, so she splashed water on to her face, ran a comb through her long dark hair, and told him she was ready.

As they went out Luke ran a finger down her smooth cold cheek. 'You look beautiful without make-up. Not all girls do.'

It was the first compliment he had ever paid her, but perversely she wouldn't show how pleased she was. 'I look terrible without lipstick,' she said ungraciously, and he gave an irritated shrug.

'Have it your way. You look terrible. Do you have to be so prickly all the time?'

'I'm not—with other people,' she panted, for Luke always took the stairs faster than anyone else. He swung round to stare at her, his dark clever face alight with amusement.

'Now that must mean something, though I'm not sure what.'

She started down the next flight ahead of him, and reached the door of his flat first. As Luke fitted his key in the door she said breathlessly, 'Don't go looking for hidden meanings. Some people just can't hit it off.'

'After you.' He waved her into his sitting-room, then busied himself with plugging in the coffee percolator in his tiny kitchen. 'I thought we'd got over all that,' he commented dryly, as he came back into the sitting-room and threw himself into a chair. 'Relax, girl. It's the only way to survive in our sort of life.'

Jill had been sitting tensely on the edge of her chair. She eased herself back a little, envying Luke's ability to stretch out like a cat. It was easy for him, she thought resentfully. *She* didn't disturb *him*. About the only feeling she aroused in Luke was a blend of irritation and amusement.

He jumped to his feet, picked up a spare cushion and plonked it behind her head. 'I said relax. You look just about all in.' He pushed her gently back in the chair. 'Do you really need to stay up? You've a busy day tomorrow.'

'She is my sister.'

'Half-sister,' he corrected sardonically.

'I want to see my father.'

His face softened. 'Of course you do. You're very fond of him, aren't you?'

She nodded, a lump suddenly in her throat. 'I see so little of him nowadays. He's my only close relative.'

Luke bent over the chair again, a hand on each of its arms, his face close to hers. 'Your relationship with your family should be different now that you've a career of your own. Have you ever thought of that?' and when she said nothing he added gently, 'You're a woman now, Jill, not a little girl. If you met your step-mother on equal terms you might be surprised at the result.'

Before she could answer the telephone rang. It was the night nurse, to say that Betty was ready for Luke's examination. He told Jill to stay where she was, and that he would send the Bentleys along to join her. 'Make them a hot drink. Whatever they fancy.'

'What a charming young man Mr Haddon is,' Marcia enthused, drinking coffee half an hour later in Luke's flat. 'So thoughtful, so kind. I'm so glad he was on duty tonight.'

'As a matter of fact he wasn't,' Jill murmured, 'and he isn't always charming, and he's only occasionally kind.' At Marcia's surprised look she added quickly, 'To us, I mean—the residents. He can be quite decent to the patients.'

Dr Bentley laughed. 'R.S.O.s don't change. The one I had was an absolute swine. Is this young man related to *Professor* Haddon, by any chance?'

When Jill told him that Luke was the old man's grandson her father was very interested, since he had been a student in the Professor's day. He told an amusing story about the great man's behaviour on a ward round, and when Jill had finished laughing she said that Luke and his grandfather were obviously similar in more than appearance.

'You've met the Professor, darling?'

Jill nodded and explained about her visits to the Haddons' house. 'But I went as Peter's guest, not Luke's,' she ended a shade wistfully, and her father gave her a keen glance.

Marcia had risen and was prowling restlessly around the room. 'I don't know how you two can be so calm. Surely it should be over by now?'

Dr Bentley tried to explain that a perforated appendix can take time, but his wife wasn't convinced. 'Doctors are always so casual when their own families are ill,' she said tartly, and rounded on Jill. 'Well, aren't I right?' she snapped. 'You're not a scrap worried about poor Betty, are you?'

Jill met the accusing stare steadily, mindful of Luke's recent remarks. 'No, I'm not worried, because I know she'll be all right. Honestly.'

Marcia sank into a chair and fidgeted with her rings. When the door opened a few minutes later and Luke walked in, she flew across the room. He took both her hands in a reassuring grip.

'She's back in bed, Mrs Bentley. She'll be fine, so you must stop worrying.'

It was a tribute to Luke's personality that Marcia did calm down. She became sufficiently relaxed to accept the fact that her husband had a job to do, and must return to Devon. For herself she would stay on at the hotel for a few days, because it was the first time Betty had ever been in hospital and the poor child was so sensitive! She must be hating every minute of it.

In fact, after the immediate post-operative discomfort, the poor child was having a wonderful time. When the residents learnt that Jill's little sister had become a patient, they looked in on her whenever they were passing and Sister would allow it. Betty had been given a small room off the main ward, and she queened it there in a variety of becoming nightdresses and bed-jackets, that her mother had insisted on buying for her on the day after the operation.

'She'll be out in a week or so,' Jill had remarked, looking with amusement at the mountain of parcels on her sister's bed.

'She needs cheering up,' Marcia demurred, watching fondly while Betty tore away tissue paper and held up a fluffy blue bed-jacket.

'Besides,' said Betty with a giggle, 'how can I impress Luke Haddon if I don't look nice?' She wriggled into the bed-jacket and examined herself in her hand-mirror with a little pout. 'I'm still very pale. Where's my make-up case?'

Useless for Jill to point out that Luke was only interested in her as a patient. Betty's vivid imagination had plenty of time to run riot.

'He's just about the most exciting man I ever met,' she enthused, on the third evening after her operation. Marcia, convinced at last that her beloved daughter was making excellent progress, had returned home, having extracted a promise from Jill that if all went as expected the two girls would travel down to Devon together the weekend after this one.

Jill, who had called in before her night round to see her young sister, wondered uneasily if Betty was making a fool of herself. On the one occasion when she had seen Luke with the girl, he had behaved like an indulgent elder brother. She tried to distract Betty's thoughts from Luke by talking about the other residents, but Betty dismissed them with a scornful wave of her hand. 'They're just boys. I'm not interested in *them.*'

'They must all be four or five years older than you,' Jill said with amusement. 'Don't waste your time weaving fantasies about Luke.'

Betty slid lower in the bed, her eyes dreamy. 'I don't think I am. I know he likes me,' and Jill, exasperated by her childishness, left the room sooner than she had intended.

At lunch two days later Luke came over to tell her that Betty had had her stitches out. 'She's ready for discharge, but Sister doesn't mind keeping her till the weekend. I understand you'll be taking her home then?'

Betty, however, had other ideas. She had heard that

there was a visitors' room in the residents' quarters, and wanted to move into it. 'I'm sick of that prissy old Sister and that bossy staff nurse!'

'Considering how kind they've been——'

'I don't want a lecture. Can I move into the visitors' room or not?'

'Perhaps it isn't free.'

'You hope,' smiled Betty. She was painting her nails, and concentrated on them for a moment while Jill stared at her in perplexity. Was there always to be antagonism between them? Wouldn't Betty ever grow up, and realise that it would be pleasanter for the whole family if they could be friends? Well, not friends, perhaps, but at least not enemies. Marcia, grateful to Jill for her help, had been unusually agreeable when she said goodbye.

Jill took a deep breath and decided to speak. 'That wasn't a very nice thing to say, especially when you're asking a favour. Why should I mind your moving in?'

Betty gave her irritating giggle. 'You don't want me poaching on your private preserves, I suppose. You were furious when I came to tea that day.'

There was just enough truth in the accusation to make Jill feel uncomfortable. 'No, I wasn't furious,' she said slowly, 'though I suppose I wasn't particularly pleased either. After all, why should I welcome you? You've never made any effort to be friendly.'

'Nor have you,' Betty retorted, and Jill sighed, knowing already that her attempt at plain speaking was going to follow the familiar pattern.

In spite of that she persisted. 'Look, Betty—couldn't we at least try to get on better? Dad would be pleased. And your mother too, I expect.'

'I said I didn't want a lecture.' Betty held out her hand and inspected it critically. 'Oh, all right, Jill! I suppose we should make more effort. So can I move into that room?' She gave the winning smile that was one of her most effective weapons.

Jill had to laugh. 'If it's free.'

'It is!' Betty said triumphantly. 'I asked one of the housemen to find out. That tall thin one with the red hair and glasses.'

'You mean Sir Angus McPherson's son?' Jill asked cunningly, for Betty was more worldly than she had been at eighteen, and likely to be impressed by a title. Archie McPherson might not match up to Luke in physical appeal, but he came from a distinguished family. Betty looked thoughtful for a moment, then returned to her main theme, for she had a one-track mind when she wanted something.

'Can I move in tomorrow morning?'

'I expect so. I'll speak to the housekeeper when she comes on duty.'

So Betty got her way and settled into the residents' quarters, and was made much of by everybody. By the men, at least : the women weren't so easy to fool. 'That little sister of yours is a menace,' Gwyneth observed, having a late cup of tea with Jill in the residents' kitchen. Everyone else had gone to bed, but the two girls were first on call, and had just come back from their wards.

Jill hoisted herself on to the table and swung her legs. 'What do you mean?'

'I mean that she likes to make trouble. This evening, when you were called away from supper, she had coffee with Peter and Luke. I heard her telling them—well, hinting anyhow—that you didn't want her here. That you'd been beastly about it.'

'Beastly' was a favourite word of Betty's. 'She likes to dramatise things,' Jill said coolly, to hide the hurt she felt at her sister's hostility. So their conversation last night had made no impact. Betty was not going to meet her half-way.

'Well, for goodness' sake!' Gwyneth cried in exasperation. 'Don't you care? Are you going to let her get away with it?'

Jill gave her friend an affectionate look. 'Of course I care, but what can I do about it? Tell Peter—and—and Luke that Betty exaggerates? That she enjoys being spiteful about me?'

'If you don't, I will.'

'Gwyneth dear, I know you mean well, but leave it alone. They're not interested in our family squabbles. They've probably forgotten all about it.'

That they didn't was partly Jill's fault, but after Gwyneth's revelations she found it difficult to maintain even a façade of friendliness towards her younger sister. At lunch she withdrew into her own thoughts, while Betty monopolised the conversation at the residents' table and kept them all in fits of laughter. Betty had inherited her mother's sharp tongue, and she had a quick if superficial wit. She loved an audience and blossomed with all the attention she was receiving.

As soon as Jill could she left the table, but as she crossed to the door Luke called to her. 'Just a moment, Jill. I want a word with you about that old chap on Lister.'

They walked out into the corridor together. Luke leant against the wall and discussed the problem of Mr Williams, and Jill did her best to concentrate on what he was saying, but as always when she was with Luke, was distracted by her emotions. When he looked at her in that intent way she found it hard to meet his eyes, which was silly when his mind was one hundred per cent on surgery, and totally devoid of any personal involvement.

'Well?' he asked impatiently, and she wrenched her thoughts back to what he was saying.

'I'm sure you're right,' she agreed weakly, and his mouth tightened.

'I don't believe you've been listening, my girl. This is important.'

She coloured. 'Yes, I know, and I am interested in Mr Williams. It's just that—that——' she put her hand to her forehead and rubbed it wearily. 'Life's been rather a strain lately. I'm a little tired.'

He looked at her searchingly, and his face softened. 'You do look washed out. Short on sleep last night?'

'I was quite busy.' The door of the dining-room opened and Betty came out with some of the residents. They went down the corridor to the common-room, laughing and talking, and Jill watched them go, unaware of how her expression had changed. Then she turned back to Luke and found that he was studying her intently.

'Why do you dislike your sister so much?' he asked quietly. 'I wouldn't have thought she rated so much hostility.'

'That's because you don't know her.' Oh, why, why had she said that? But when she was with Luke she never behaved sensibly.

He gave an irritated shrug. 'Is there anything to know? She's just a silly little girl.' He thought for a moment and added words that would have infuriated Betty even more. 'I expect she'll marry young and make some poor devil unhappy for the rest of his life!'

So at least Luke wasn't fooled by Betty, which showed that he was shrewder than most of his sex. Jill never ceased to be amazed at the way clever men could fall for pretty girls, who were totally devoid of brains. Was Karen cleverer than she seemed, or was her physical appeal so great that it simply didn't matter?

She came out of this reverie when Luke tapped her on the shoulder. 'Why are you so dreamy these days? Half the time you seem lost to the world.'

She flushed and moved away from him, unable to

sustain the inquiry in those dark intelligent eyes. 'I. need a break, I expect. Thank goodness it's my week-end off.'

On Friday afternoon Jill went to her room to pack her weekend case. She wasn't off duty till five, so rather than having to rush to the station, the girls had de-cided to travel on the overnight sleeper train. When the telephone rang it was Luke.

'I'm having a few people in for drinks this evening. Can you and your sister come?'

Jill reminded him that they were off to Devon for the weekend.

'What time is your train? Then you can make it for an hour or so. Peter will run you to the station, I ex-pect.'

Betty was delighted when she heard of this invita-tion, and insisted that Luke must be giving her a send-off. 'What a pity I can't wear something really exotic and sexy! Though I suppose I could change back quickly.'

'You could not,' Jill said firmly, 'and I shouldn't think for a moment that it's in your honour. He's just being friendly, that's all.'

But Betty persisted in her delusion until they walked into Luke's flat and heard the news. Karen's father was returning unexpectedly to California.

'Business problems,' she told Jill unconcernedly, 'so I thought I'd go along and soak up some sunshine. I've had enough for the present of your English winter!'

The freezing weather had in no way dimmed Karen's extraordinary beauty. She glowed with health and vitality, outshining every other woman in the room. Betty, after one incredulous stare, had edged her way into a corner and was doing her best to charm the previously despised Archie McPherson. Her sharp ears had undoubtedly caught Luke's remark to some-

one about meeting the guest of honour, as he led the
man over to the American girl's side.

'But I'll be back soon, honey,' Karen promised gaily,
sliding a hand through his arm and smiling up at him.
They made a striking pair, the dark head and the
golden one close together, sharing some joke that Jill
couldn't quite hear. Luke didn't look unhappy at
the prospect of Karen's departure, but Karen had said
she would soon be back. The air fare for a five-
thousand-mile trip meant nothing to a millionaire's
daughter.

'Do you think they'll get engaged before she leaves?'
Jill asked Peter, who had manoeuvred her into a
corner of the room and was trying to talk about himself.

Peter looked irritated. 'Did you hear a word I said?
I've missed you.'

'Missed me?' Jill asked, puzzled. 'What do you
mean?'

He let out an exasperated sigh. 'Oh, I know you've
been around, but I haven't been alone with you for
ages.' He took hold of her hands and gave them a
little shake. 'Do you have to go home this weekend? Couldn't we put your sister on the train and your
family can meet her the other end? She's only had an
appendectomy, for God's sake.'

'Yes, I know, but her mother fusses. And I promised.'

'Oh, all right,' he said sulkily, 'but I thought, as
we're both off, that we might have done something together.'

'I'm sorry,' Jill said, smiling at his glum face, 'but
you know you'll find a substitute, so don't look so fed
up!'

He twitched the curtain back and gazed down at the
deserted street. 'It's foggy. We mustn't leave it too
late if you insist on catching that train.'

Jill was watching Luke and Karen again. She would

make a determined effort not to stare and keep it up for a minute or two, but her eyes kept coming back to them, and she couldn't resist repeating her earlier question.

'Do you think they'll get engaged?'

'How should I know?' Peter snapped with quite unusual bad temper. 'Luke doesn't discuss his love life with me. Grandma hopes he won't, at any rate.'

So Karen had been down to the Haddons' place, which was scarcely surprising. 'But how could anyone not take to her?' Jill asked, for though she envied Karen she couldn't dislike her.

'Grandma thinks she's wrong for Luke,' Peter said without much interest, slid an arm around her waist and piloted her across the room. 'And Grandpa hates Americans,' he hissed in her ear.

Jill laughed. 'That's very intolerant of him!'

They had halted on the edge of the group around Karen and Luke. 'He is intolerant,' Peter said with a grin, 'and gets worse as he gets older. He likes you, though. He was asking when you'll be down again.'

'That's nice,' Jill said absently, because she was trying to hear what Luke was saying. He looked their way suddenly, smiled and moved towards tthem. She stiffened and brushed a nervous hand over her hair.

'Peter looking after you? Have you time for another drink?'

'No, we haven't.' She was abrupt because she was so afraid of showing her feelings for him. Peter, his arm still around her waist, gave her a puzzled glance, and Luke raised his eyebrows.

'Getting edgy about that train? You've plenty of time.'

'I'd like to go, just the same.'

'Karen,' Luke called, 'come and say goodbye to Jill.'

The American girl was charming, warm and friendly

and genuine. When she said she hoped they would meet again she meant it. 'Dad will have to come back. Business!' Karen grimaced. 'It's all he thinks about.' Then she gave her wide smile. 'But it gives me the chance to travel in style! Nothing but the best for my old man!'

She included Betty in her farewell, a rather subdued Betty, who remained quieter than usual on the way to the station. In the sleeper, preparing for bed, she looked preoccupied. She was removing her eye make-up before she came to life again, and startled Jill with her sudden exclamation.

'It's not fair, no one else has a chance!' At Jill's enquiring look she added viciously, 'Looking like that. And all that money. And did you see that dress? It's not fair!'

'Life isn't fair,' Jill agreed with a faint smile. 'Some people do seem to be luckier than others, Betty. You just have to accept it.'

Betty sank down on the bottom bunk. 'You were right about Luke,' she said sadly. 'He hardly spoke to me all evening, he was so taken up with her.'

'But Archie McPherson did,' Jill murmured, hoping to deflect her little sister's thoughts in a more cheerful direction. 'He likes you very much, I'm sure of it.'

Betty shrugged. 'Oh, Archie! I suppose he's better than no one. He wants to come and see me on his next free weekend. His family have a cottage near Salcombe.'

Salcombe was only thirty miles from their home. 'Good,' said Jill brightly. 'That'll be fun.'

Betty didn't bother to answer. She climbed into the bunk in her slip and lay on her back, staring upwards. Jill cleaned her teeth and washed. She was drying her face when Betty spoke again.

'You fancy him too, don't you?'

Jill caught her breath and became absolutely still, the towel on her cheek. Then she let out her breath and started to rub vigorously.

'Don't do that to your face,' said Betty. 'You'll ruin your complexion.' Betty at eighteen was a great one for skin care.

Jill turned from the washbasin, her face flushed, but perhaps Betty would think it was due to that vigorous rubbing. 'I'm not with you,' she managed with elaborate casualness.

Betty propped herself up on one elbow and studied her older sister with interest. 'Oh yes, you are, Jill. You can't fool me. I was watching you tonight, and *you* were watching Luke. It was a dead giveaway.'

Jill avoided her sister's eyes and climbed into the top bunk. 'You're being silly, Betty. I'm going to sleep.' She snapped off her light and a moment or two later Betty put out hers.

Then her breathy little girl voice floated up from the lower bunk. 'Funny! We've never fancied the same man before. I wonder if Peter noticed it? Probably that was why he looked so fed up.'

CHAPTER EIGHT

'HAVE a good time?' Peter asked on Monday.

'A good time?'

'At home?'

'Oh. Yes, all right.' Jill spoke without much enthusiasm. Then the first patient was wheeled down the theatre corridor and they parted to their respective changing rooms.

It had not been all right. She had had anything but a good time, though her stepmother had greeted her with more warmth than usual and her father, as a result, had appeared more relaxed.

'It was good of you to look after Betty so well.' Marcia's usual perfunctory smile had been replaced by one of genuine friendliness. 'I hope she didn't lose her head with all those young men around!'

Jill laughed. 'She had a super time. There's safety in numbers, after all.'

She thought that Betty's infatuation for Luke was just a passing fancy. The girl was too immature emotionally, too avid for masculine admiration, to waste long pining over a man who wasn't interested in her. She had told her mother about Archie McPherson, and Marcia was delighted when she heard that the young man's father had a title.

'You must ask him round, darling, if he does come down.'

'He will,' said Betty confidently. The girl had recovered her good humour, though she couldn't resist the occasional sly dig at her sister. Jill was convinced that Betty gained considerable satisfaction from the thought that Luke was not for either of them. She would have been downright spiteful if Luke had evinced the least interest in Jill at the party.

So Jill hadn't enjoyed her weekend break and was glad to be back at work. She was in that unhappy state when she knew that her love was hopeless, and yet longed to be near the man she loved, to see him, to speak to him occasionally, to hear others talk about him. She despised herself for her weakness, but lacked the strength of will to do anything about it.

'Is something wrong?' Gwyneth asked one day. 'You've been different lately.'

Jill denied this vehemently. 'I've been working very hard.'

'We all work very hard,' her friend countered, and subjected Jill to a thoughtful look. 'Are you sure you don't mind Peter going off?'

Peter was leaving at the weekend for two weeks' skiing in Switzerland. A party went each year from the hospital, though Jill had never been with them. Peter had tried to talk her into going this time, but Jill had pointed out that she didn't ski.

'You could learn,' he had muttered. 'It will be the first time for several of them.'

Gwyneth was going, and Gwyneth had never been before. 'I don't suppose I shall be any good,' she said cheerfully. 'I've always been clumsy, but it will be fun trying. I wish you were coming.'

Jill was glad that she wasn't, for a break from Peter would be most welcome. He seemed reluctant to admit defeat. He hung about her, behaved possessively, made excuses to come to her room. Behaved, in short, like a man in love, though Jill had decided that he was motivated more by pride than affection. Peter had always been successful with women, and he didn't like to be turned down.

Thre was a locum for Peter, a bouncy cheerful young man from another hospital, who didn't hit it off well with Luke. He grumbled to Jill about the R.S.O.'s awkward disposition and Jill listened sympathetically, because though she loved Luke she wasn't blind to his faults.

'I know he can be difficult,' she agreed over a mid-morning coffee, 'but he'll be finishing this job at the end of the month. You'll only have one week of him.' Her voice wavered as she said this, but William Young didn't seem to notice.

'That's not what I heard,' he said glumly. 'He's been asked to stay on for another three months.'

Jill's heavy heart lightened at this news, and she flashed him a smile that made him blink. 'You'll get used to him. I did.'

'Never,' William exclaimed, glanced round as several people entered the dining-room, and put his mouth close to Jill's ear. 'Talk of the devil! Let's hope he sits at another table.'

However, Luke chose to settle himself right opposite, though he was engaged in discussing some surgical problem and paid no attention to them. He did look up when they left, his eyes travelling from Jill to William, then back to Jill, in a way that brought a flush to her cheeks.

'So he needles you too,' William observed as they walked down the corridor. 'Why was he looking at you like that?'

Jill shrugged and turned the conversation to less personal matters, though she had been puzzled herself by Luke's expression.

That evening she was curled up in an easy chair, watching television, when Luke came into the room. He helped himself to coffee and sat down beside her.

'Heard from Peter?' he asked.

'No, of course not.'

'Why of course not?' he queried sardonically, and she looked back at him levelly, relieved that she could appear so calm.

'I shouldn't think Peter is much of a correspondent.'

'True,' he agreed with a faint smile, 'but people act out of character when they're in love.'

The film was a Western and noisy. Under cover of the gunfight Jill told Luke that he was being ridiculous, that Peter was not in love with her, and that she most certainly didn't love him. Luke urged her to calm down; if she wanted to be cagey about her affairs he quite understood. He sipped his coffee and didn't speak again, but Jill was conscious of his eyes on her. When she rose to go on her night round he followed her out into the corridor.

'It is your half day tomorrow? Have you anything on?' When she shook her head he laid a hand on her arm and brought her to a halt. 'I was thinking of paying a visit to my grandparents. Care to come?'

He spoke so casually that it was easy to be casual in return. It would be wonderful to spend some time alone with him, whatever his motive for asking her. Perhaps he missed Karen and thought that she too, in spite of her protests, was missing his brother. Perhaps it had been one of those spur-of-the-moment invitations, and anyway it didn't matter. He had asked, she had accepted and she would make the most of it, for she was unlikely ever again to be invited out by Luke.

They left Q.C.H. at midday, because Luke in his high-handed way had talked one of the other house surgeons into covering for Jill. Commanded had been more like it, Jill thought with amusement.

'You're bad enough as R.S.O.,' she told him over lunch, 'you'll be terrible as a consultant!'

They were sitting in the lounge of an old country pub, tucked away in a corner beside a roaring fire. Jill left pleasantly relaxed, and joyfully aware of a whole half day to be spent in Luke's company. She knew there was no future in it, but she was determined to enjoy the present.

When Luke expressed himself baffled by her remark, she explained, 'I shouldn't really have been off till one. We could have eaten in hospital.'

'Much nicer here, though.' Luke smiled, stretching out his long legs and taking a bite out of his ham sandwich.

They talked easily and Jill was struck again by the similarity of their tastes; it was their temperaments that seemed so incompatible. Lulled by the comfortable surroundings and his unusually benign manner, she was unwise enough to speculate aloud.

'I wonder why we don't get on better. We have so much in common.'

She regretted this remark when Luke gave her one of his most irritating smiles. 'Only off duty, my dear Jill. If you're in a mood for analysis, which is probably unwise, I'd say you're anti-authority, just for the hell of it.'

'No, I'm not. I get on very well with Sir James, unlike the rest of his firm.'

'That,' said Luke dryly, 'is because he likes pretty girls. You could get away with murder there—and often do.'

She coloured. 'Let's drop it. I don't know how we started this.'

Luke took a long slow drink of his beer. 'You started it.' He gave her that intent stare that so disconcerted her. 'There are of course other reasons for our mutual ... antipathy?' He added the last word as a question.

This was dangerous ground. Still flushed, Jill cast about for a safer topic and came up with a query. Was it true that he was staying on longer than had originally been planned? Quite true, he said, with one of his most maddening smiles. The R.S.O. had asked for extended study leave. 'So I'll outlast you. Bad luck, my girl,' but the smile was less sarcastic now. He was teasing her gently and she responded lightheartedly.

He told her that his grandparents were delighted

that she was coming down again, and the welcome she received from them was clear proof of this. They sat around the fire in the small sitting-room which they used when they were on their own, and Jill felt almost one of the family. She listened to Luke and his grandfather discussing some controversial surgical problem, and thought wistfully that this was probably the last time she would ever come to this lovely house. Her eyes went to Luke, sprawled at the other end of the sofa, his lanky body relaxed, but his mind, as ever, sharp and questioning. He flung a question at his grandfather and followed it up with a smile, as if he knew he'd stumped the old man, and was pleased to have done so.

Professor Haddon looked almost annoyed, then amused. 'You're right, my boy, though I hate to admit it.' He turned to Jill, the smile still lingering on his lean features. 'And how's this lad behaving as R.S.O.? Making himself unpopular?'

'R.S.O.s are always unpopular,' Luke drawled before Jill could think of an answer, and Mrs Haddon leant forward to contribute a remark.

'Then they shouldn't be. Couldn't you try to be more ... approachable, Luke?'

Luke shrugged and laughed, and was still smiling when he went off with Professor Haddon to the library, to settle their argument by a reference to some medical journal. Mrs Haddon stared after them, her forehead puckered. 'He's such a dear boy,' she murmured, 'but he hasn't yet learnt humility.'

'I doubt if he ever will,' said Jill. 'It's—not really a family characteristic, is it?'

The old lady sighed. 'I suppose not. He's so like my husband at that age.' Another sigh. 'Luke's been too successful, I think. Do you understand what I mean?'

This was a surprising remark from a loving grandmother, and a credit to Mrs Haddon's intelligence.

'Yes,' Jill said slowly, 'I think I do,' and then their talk became less intimate, and soon after Luke returned, followed by the dogs. He leant over the back of Jill's chair.

'Care for a walk? We've just time before tea.'

Mrs Haddon glanced out of the window at the grey and frozen landscape. 'It's a horrible day and it's nearly dark. I'm sure Jill would rather sit by the fire.'

'Jill needs some exercise,' her grandson said firmly, pulling the girl up from her chair by both hands, and as they made for the door Jill threw a laughing remark over her shoulder at Mrs Haddon.

'You were right! He's quite impossible!'

'What was that about?' Luke asked as he helped her into her coat. 'Discussing me with Grandma?' His hands tightened on her shoulders and he gave her a little shake, but he looked amused, not annoyed. As they set off down the drive, their feet crunching on the icy patches, he said thoughtfully that he was darned if he knew how she did it—his grandfather had quite lost his heart to her. 'They'll be very disappointed if you don't marry Peter.'

'We've had this conversation before,' Jill pointed out, 'and I'm sorry, but they'll just have to be disappointed.' She dug her hands deeper into her pockets and put her head down against the bitter wind. 'Please, Luke, I don't want to talk about Peter.'

'O.K.,' Luke said amicably, and they trudged on silently, but with an unusually comfortable feeling between them.

Luke had intended leaving as soon as dinner was over, but they lingered over coffee, and it was ten o'clock before they were in the car. No one had looked out of the windows during the evening, so they were surprised to find a light fall of snow. As they turned on to the A21 it began to snow again, lightly at first and then more thickly, so that it clogged the windscreen wipers. Luke swore and stopped the car in a lay-by to clear the windscreen more effectively, and when he got back into the car his dark hair was flecked with white.

'Shouldn't we wait till it slackens off?' Jill suggested, but he shook his head.

'It could go on for hours, and I don't fancy being benighted in this godforsaken spot. Let's at least get to the next village.'

There were no other cars in the lay-by, and they passed no more than half a dozen as they crawled along with frequent halts. Luke let out a long sigh of relief when they saw lights in the distance, blurred and distorted by the falling snow.

'There's a nice old pub on the outskirts of this place. We'll stop there ... for the night if necessary.'

Several other people had had the same idea, so the few bedrooms were already occupied, but the publican told them that they were welcome to spend the night in the saloon bar. There was already another couple there, a young man and a girl, in motor-cyclists' gear. They had drawn one of the oak settles up to the open fire, and sat, entwined and loving, paying little attention to the newcomers after a few casual words about the filthy weather. The publican's wife brought them hot drinks, coffee laced with whisky, and while they sipped it appreciatively Jill asked Luke if he intended driving on, should the snow stop.

'Not on your life, it's freezing hard. We'll wait till morning. What have you got on tomorrow? A ward round? Then we'll leave early, but if we get held up you'll have to ring them and say you'll be late.' He finished his coffee and slanted her a quizzical smile. 'This'll set the grapevine buzzing! You and I having a night out together!'

Jill was annoyed with herself for blushing. 'Don't be silly,' she said with unusual primness. 'And anyway, who'll know?'

Luke rested his head against the back of the settee and regarded her through half-closed eyes. 'Someone always knows. It's incredible how things get around at Queen's. Who was seen coming out of whose bedroom before breakfast!' he quirked an eyebrow at her. 'Perhaps it's the sparrows?'

Jill laughed and agreed that hospital gossip spread at a truly astonishing speed. She stared into the fire and her eyelids drooped. 'You're tired,' Luke said gently. 'This settle is damned uncomfortable, so you'd better lean against me,' and before she knew what he was doing she was in the curve of his arm, her head resting against his chest. 'Relax,' he murmured, after a minute or two, and then rather dryly, 'You can pretend I'm Peter if you like.'

'I've already told you——'

'Yes, I know.' He gave a little tug at her hair. 'Stop arguing. I'm tired too,' so she did her best to relax, staring into the fire and pretending, not that Luke was Peter, but that he was himself, and in love with her, holding her close because it was the natural thing to do. She knew that she was being foolish and smiled to herself at Luke's reaction if he could have guessed her thoughts. The settle was uncomfortable and she was sure that she would stay awake all night, but before long she drifted off, and woke with a start to find Luke shifting her away from him.

The young couple who had shared the room with them were preparing to leave. Crash helmets in hand, they were exchanging a few words with Luke.

'If we get stuck we'll hitch a lift from you, mate,' the lad said, gave a friendly grin and slouched through the door.

'What time is it?' Jill asked sleepily.

'Just gone seven. I can hear sounds upstairs. I hope that means they're early risers.'

Jill stretched and stood up rather stiffly. She was

sure she must look a mess and would have liked to look in a mirror, but wasn't going to do it in front of Luke. She smoothed her hair down, feeling self-conscious when she remembered the night.

'Stop fussing,' said Luke, 'you look very sweet.' He crossed to her side, a gleam in his dark eyes that set her heart pounding. 'You're not one of those girls who look terrible first thing in the morning,' he added softly. Jill stared up at him, incapable of any rejoinder, overwhelmed by his closeness and the strength of his physical attraction. Slowly Luke put out a hand, taking her by one shoulder. Then his grip tightened and his expression changed, until he looked tense and almost angry. 'We could do with some breakfast,' he said abruptly, let her go and strode through the door.

Jill's knees were trembling and her breathing was rapid. She knew why Luke was annoyed; because for a few moments he had felt the pull of mutual attraction, and hated to admit it. In his case it had probably been as transient as it was unwelcome. Thank goodness that she had a breathing space in which to pull herself together!

By the time Luke came back Jill had washed and done her face, and even more important, recovered her composure. He was accompanied by the landlady with a tray of bacon and eggs, tea and toast. They ate quickly and in silence, then Luke went off to settle the bill. As they picked their way through deep snow to the car, Jill offered to pay her share, a remark which Luke treated with disdain.

The sun was shining now and the whole world sparkled. A good deal of traffic had already passed along the main road, so that driving was easier than it had been last night. Luke glanced at his watch. 'Unless it's worse nearer London we shouldn't be very late.'

Jill stole a quick look at him. He drove carefully, concentrating on the road, and seemed disinclined to talk. 'Fine,' she thought, 'I'm not in a chatty mood either.' She spent most of the journey wondering if she had given herself away to Luke back there in the pub. If so, that would account for his air of moodiness. Men hated women who couldn't contain their emotions.

They ran into heavy traffic on the outskirts of London, so that it was ten-thirty when they turned into the hospital car park. 'Let's have a quick coffee before we start work,' suggested Luke. When they walked into the hospital dining-room there were quite a few people already there. Sir James, sitting with William Young and Bill Mackie, looked at them over the top of his spectacles, and beckoned them to his table.

'I hear you were snowed up, my boy,' he rumbled. 'Down in Sussex I believe, at your grandfather's place?'

'At a pub near Tonbridge, actually,' Luke said easily. 'We started back to London last night, but we had to give up.'

William pulled out a chair for Jill, while Luke went to fetch their coffee.

'I'm sorry to be so late, Sir James, but we really couldn't make it last night.'

'No need to apologise, my dear child. I'm sure it was unavoidable.' Sir James pushed his spectacles on to the bridge of his nose, and his small shrewd eyes considered her carefully. 'And how is my old friend David Haddon?'

She made some rejoinder, aware that a good many people had stared at Luke and her when they came in together. Word must have got around already about last night, and Jill wished Luke hadn't felt it necessary to telephone his stand-in from the pub. She did her best to appear casual and unconcerned, but perhaps she wasn't very successful, for Luke eyed her thoughtfully more than once, though he said nothing.

William had no such inhibitions. 'What's with you and Luke Haddon?' he asked, when they were walking back to the residents' quarters at the end of the morning. 'I thought you didn't like him.'

Jill coloured and stared straight ahead. 'I never said that. I said he could be difficult.'

'But you're prepared to put up with him because of his position? And his prospects,' William suggested cynically, and her colour deepened.

'Do stop being silly. It's not like that at all.'

William wasn't the only one, however. Jill had to put up with a lot of ribbing, most of it good-natured, during the next few days. 'That American bird of his won't like it,' said one of the house surgeons, and someone else added, 'I should stick to Sir James! He's easier to handle!'

There was a good deal of laughter at this, and Jill did her best to take it with a good grace, but her patience was wearing thin. She ate her meals quickly and stayed away from the common-room, avoiding any confrontation with Luke. She thought it unlikely that anyone had had the temerity to make similar remarks to *him*! After a few days the gossip died down, and then it was time for the skiing party to return. They came back with deep tans, pleased with themselves and the success of their holiday.

'It was super,' Gwyneth told Jill, 'you must try it some time.'

Jill had called in to see her friend, who was in the middle of unpacking with clothes scattered everywhere. The only place to sit was on the bed, so Jill perched on the edge and listened to the Welsh girl's enthusiastic chatter. When she had finished talking about her affairs, she asked Jill what had been going on in her absence. 'I mean, you and Luke? Is it really true?' Her lively face was alight with curiosity and amusement.

'Heavens, Gwyneth, I shouldn't have expected even you to pick it up that quickly!' snapped Jill. 'Besides, it's not particularly interesting. I thought everyone had forgotten about it.'

'You and Luke Haddon out on a date!' exclaimed Gwyneth, refusing to be put off that easily. 'I was staggered, I can tell you. Come on, why were you out all night? Do tell.'

Reluctantly Jill explained and Gwyneth listened, then nodded. 'Well, of course I didn't think there was anything in it. I just wanted to know. But what made you go out with him in the first place?'

'I was free that afternoon,' Jill sighed, 'and so was he, so he asked me. We were both at a loose end, I suppose. Don't go making a big thing of it, please.'

'And Peter? What does he say?'

'I've hardly spoken to Peter since he came back,' Jill said dismissively, but Gwyneth wouldn't take the hint.

'Perhaps he doesn't care, one way or the other. He was pretty wrapped up in that blonde staff nurse on Jenner while we were away. You know, the one he used to date before he took up with you.'

'Delighted to hear it,' Jill said firmly, and left Gwyneth to her unpacking. Peter's behaviour was scarcely surprising, since he had been cool towards her before he left. He was polite but distant when they met over work, and had made no attempt to get in touch with her since his return. If he had gone back to his staff nurse that was good news to Jill.

Later that evening she was sitting in her room when someone tapped on her door. She called 'Come in,' and turned to see Luke. She stared at him in surprise, and became, as so often in his presence, bereft of speech.

Luke crossed the room and indicated the other chair. 'May I?' She nodded. 'If you're busy this won't take long.' Jill turned her radio off, fiddling with the knobs for something to do. 'Why have you been avoiding me?'

Her head jerked up at that. 'I ... haven't.'

'Of course you have,' he said quietly. 'When you saw me coming down the corridor this afternoon you bolted like a scared rabbit. And you've hardly been in the common-room for days. Why, Jill?'

She shifted uncomfortably in her chair, wishing she had the sophistication to deal with him more casually. 'People have been saying silly things. About that night when we got stuck at the pub.'

His look of astonishment changed to one of scorn. 'You mean to say that's why you've been avoiding me?'

She stared at the fire. 'They embarrassed me with their stupid jokes.'

'So you've been hiding in here.' His voice was suddenly gentle and faintly amused. 'I thought you were tougher than that. You should be, after five years of medical school.' His expression was quizzical. He lounged opposite her, long legs stretched towards the fire, head resting on the back of the chair, the most attractive man she had ever met, and made more so when he smiled at her like that. 'You've been avoiding Peter too?'

'No. He's been avoiding me.'

'Why should he do that?'

'Well ... perhaps avoiding's the wrong word. I think he's finally got the message—that we're not—well—really suited to each other.'

'I see,' Luke said softly, and suddenly he was sitting forward in his chair and regarding her intently.

'And don't tell me your grandparents will be very disappointed,' Jill said, trying for the light touch, because he made her nervous when he stared at her like that.

He smiled. 'Grandma won't, because she's changed her mind about you.' He waited for her reaction, but she said nothing, though she felt rather hurt, for the old lady had been so friendly on her last visit. 'Don't you want to know why?' Luke asked.

'Not particularly.'

'I'll tell you just the same. Give you a good laugh, since you're looking rather down. Grandma, bless her, thinks *we* are right for each other. You and I!'

Jill's astonishment was so great that she felt no embarrassment. Luke laughed at her reaction and rose to his feet. 'It's O.K., Jill. Grandma sees life from a peculiar angle. I must have put the idea in her head when I took you down,' and still laughing he moved towards the door. He stopped suddenly, as if remembering the original purpose of his visit. 'The best way to cope with gossip is to ignore it. Tell them to go to hell!'

When he had gone Jill sat deep in thought, miles away in Sussex, going over in her mind that last visit to the Haddons'. It was a bittersweet remembrance, a form of self-indulgence, because she didn't want to think of Luke's laughter when he told her his grandmother's views.

If only Luke didn't have a girl-friend. If only he had shown even a flicker of interest in her tonight. That morning at the pub he had been momentarily attracted, though he had probably forgotten all about it.

'I wish he wasn't staying on. I wish I was finishing sooner,' Jill said aloud, then surprised herself by bursting into tears.

CHAPTER NINE

THOUGH Peter was back at work William Young stayed on, to do a month's locum for another registrar who was taking study leave. He was no longer on Sir James' firm, but he was becoming increasingly friendly with Jill. The first time he asked her out he issued the invitation in a typical William manner.

'Care to go slumming tonight? If you've nothing better to do, of course.' William, like Gwyneth, had a bit of a chip on his shoulder, because he didn't come from an educated family, and was lacking in polish. Jill liked him and was sorry for him, not because of his background, but because he minded so much about it.

They got in the habit of sitting for hours in coffee bars or pubs, while William poured out his heart to her, and she did her best to bolster up his self-confidence. 'The most I can hope for is a consultant job in some dreary town, where no one else wants to go.' He had said this before, with variations, on a number of occasions.

'Oh, stop it!' Jill cried. 'Snap out of it!' Sympathy hadn't helped, so she decided to be blunt. 'The only thing that will stop you reaching the top is yourself. You've brains and ability, but all too often you rub people up the wrong way.'

'That's my lack of breeding,' William said belligerently.

'Oh, William!' Jill laughed at him gently, and he smiled reluctantly.

'All right then, I'm just naturally aggressive.'

'You could learn not to be. Are you going to apply for that senior registrar's job?'

William shook his head. 'No point, it's earmarked

for Luke Haddon. The golden boy of Q.C.H.' His expression was disagreeable, for poor William envied and disliked the other man.

This was news to Jill. 'Has he applied for it?'

'So the rumour goes, and of course he'll get it. What went wrong between you and Peter Haddon?'

'There was nothing to go wrong,' Jill said with reserve, and he grinned back at her.

'Gwyneth says you could have had him if you'd wanted. She thinks you're just too unworldly to be true.'

'Gwyneth talks too much.'

'But she's shrewd. With Haddon as a boy-friend you could have gone right to the top.'

'Thanks, but I'd rather succeed on merit—or not at all.' She meant that most sincerely, but was afraid it sounded smug.

William didn't seem to think so. He leant towards her and put a large square hand over her small one. 'You're very sweet, Jill. Quite the nicest girl I know.' Then he looked up and scowled. 'Hallo, Haddon—Smithies.'

Jill turned quickly. Luke and another registrar were standing by their table. 'Mind if we join you?' Luke asked pleasantly. The pub was crowded and there was nowhere else to sit. William nodded ungraciously, shifting along the bench seat, so that he was very close to Jill. Luke slid into the place opposite her and apologised for disturbing them. His words were innocuous, but his expression wasn't. Jill avoided his eyes and talked determinedly to Mr Smithies, since William had relapsed into silence. After a few minutes he rose to go.

'No point staying once *they* came,' he grumbled. 'Why are you always so edgy with that chap?'

She didn't pretend to misunderstand him. 'Luke and I—we've never really hit it off.'

'Sort of love-hate relationship?' William joked, sliding an arm through hers as they walked back through the side streets to the hospital.

'Don't be idiotic!' She pulled her arm away, but William attached himself to her again, this time more closely.

'Not silly. Don't the psychologists'—he stumbled a little over the word—'say the two aren't far apart?'

'You've had too much to drink.' Thank goodness they were nearly back! William wasn't usually a heavy drinker, but he'd tossed back two whiskies after the others joined them, maybe to bolster his self-confidence. He had once confessed to Jill that the chaps from Cambridge, with their snooty accents, made him feel inferior.

When they reached the residency Jill made him a cup of strong coffee. The common-room was empty for the moment; probably most of the residents on duty were doing their night rounds, and the ones who were off were still out. William sat beside her on the sofa and put an arm round her. He smelt strongly of whisky and his face was flushed.

'Please stop it!'

But he was stronger than she was and she couldn't push him away. If she allowed him to kiss her perhaps he would let her go. He planted a clumsy kiss on her mouth, fumbling at her clothing, and Jill reacted violently to that. 'Let me go, William! Let me go!'

Her distaste must have got through to him, for he drew away, looking sulky. In the morning, if he remembered, he would probably be embarrassed, for William didn't usually behave like this. 'Not good enough for you, am I?' he asked unpleasantly.

Jill jumped to her feet. 'Drink your coffee and go to bed. It was those last two Scotches on top of all the rest, I'm afraid.'

'Are you implying I'm drunk? Never been drunk in

my life,' muttered William. 'You wouldn't push away
the high and mighty Luke, if *he* wanted to make love
to you.' She gasped a protest, but he paid no attention.
'I'm not blind—or dim. I saw the way you reacted
when he joined us.'

'Please stop, William.' Jill glanced nervously towards the door, afraid that someone would come in
and overhear.

'I won't stop it,' said William with increasing trucu-
lence. 'I know now why you ditched his brother. You
think Luke has more to offer.' He negotiated these
sentences with some difficulty.

'You've got it all wrong,' Jill cried. 'I just ... like
Luke better,' and that was a crazy admission to William in his present state.

'Of course you do,' sneered William, totally trans-
formed from his usual friendly self. 'They're both
heading for the top, but Luke will get there first. No,
you most certainly wouldn't push *him* away!'

As angry as he was now, Jill snapped back, 'At least
he's sober, which makes him a whole lot more attractive than you!' She gave him a look of disgust and
turned towards the door, but before she could reach it
Luke and Jim Smithies came in.

'Has anyone made coffee?' Luke asked, took in Jill's
flushed face and untidy hair, and glanced sardonically
at William. William, thank goodness, had hunched
himself on the sofa, fuddled and morose, and looked as
if he would be asleep any moment.

'Good—goodnight,' Jill stammered, and rushed
from the room. Only when she looked at herself in her
bedroom mirror did she realise that the top three
buttons of her blouse were undone, and her face
flamed, realising what Luke must have thought.

'You certainly stirred things up last night,' Gwyneth
observed next day, and proceeded to enlarge. She had
walked into the common-room to find William lying

on the floor and Luke standing over him. 'As if he'd just knocked him down,' Gwyneth said with evident enjoyment, for she hadn't taken to their locum registrar. 'Then he hauled William to his feet and shook him hard. Told him to shut up or else!'

Jill bit her lip. 'And ... did William say anything——'

'He certainly did! About it being all your fault. You'd led him on, then let him down with a bang.' Gwyneth eyed her friend speculatively. 'And one other things, but perhaps I'd better not repeat that.'

'Please, Gwyneth, tell me the worst.'

'He said something about you being one for the main chance. Told Luke you wouldn't push *him* away, so why didn't he make a play for you? You'd admitted you were after him.'

'Oh, no!' Jill whispered, dropped on to Gwyneth's bed and put her face in her hands.

'He was drunk, of course,' Gwyneth said, attempting consolation. 'I'm sorry, Jill, but you did ask.'

'I'll never be able to face Luke again. I feel so ashamed.'

'Well, for goodness' sake! You didn't really say that? I thought he was making it up.'

'Not entirely,' Jill said miserably. 'I mean, we did talk about Luke, and I—I more or less agreed when William said I wouldn't have minded Luke kissing me.'

Gwyneth's eyes widened. 'So it was true! No wonder Luke looked so furious.'

'What happened in the end?'

'Well, I was standing in the doorway, taking it all in, when Luke spotted me. He sort of demolished me with a look. You know how he can be?' Yes, Jill did know, and dreaded the moment when he would look at her like that. 'Told me that if I said one word I'd live to regret it, but I don't think he could mind my telling you.' Gwyneth gave a jerky laugh. 'Then they carted William off to bed. That's all.'

'All!' sighed Jill despairingly.

Gwyneth dropped down beside her and gave her an affectionate hug. 'It does have its funny side.'

'Not to me. I must go round the wards.'

'You haven't had breakfast yet.'

'I don't feel hungry,' objected Jill.

'You'll have to meet them some time.'

'Yes, I know, but not just yet.' She saw both Luke and William at lunch, but they were at the registrars' table. At opposite ends, she noted, and neither looked her way.

Luke came on Sir James' ward round next day, but acted as if she didn't exist.

'What's wrong, love?' Mrs Christie asked, when Jill stayed behind in the ward to write up some drugs. 'You look proper poorly.'

'I didn't sleep.' That was true enough, for she had lain awake, wretched and apprehensive, trying to make up her mind if she should or shouldn't say something to Luke. William had already approached her and mumbled an apology, but Jill couldn't really blame him. It had been her fault entirely, for not concealing her feelings better, and for making indiscreet remarks, which he would never have repeated if he had been sober.

She was off for the weekend, but she didn't look forward to it with any pleasure. Time dragged by, and on Sunday afternoon she went for a long walk in Regent's Park, because walking always made her feel better when she was overwrought. Anything, anything would be better than having Luke look through her as if she didn't exist. So he might snub her, swear at her, treat her with contempt; anything would be better than being ignored. He was on duty today, so she would try and talk to him when she got back—apologise, explain William's remarks away as the exaggeration of a drunken man, which to some extent they had been.

She had walked farther than she realised and it was nearly dusk. The lights of Marylebone Road twinkled in the distance as she trudged back through the park, tired now, but calm. She went into the dining-room and had a cup of tea to warm herself up, but didn't eat anything or talk to the few people who were still there. Then she went up to her room and picked up the telephone. Luke didn't answer. She sank wearily into her chair, waited ten minutes and tried again. On the third attempt he answered, and she nearly jammed the receiver down in panic. So much for her hard-won calm! She swallowed and asked if he was on his own.

A short pause. 'Yes,' he said curtly.

'Can I—can I come and see you?'

'What about?'

'I—I'd rather not discuss it on the phone.'

'Not to do with work?'

'N-no.'

'Then don't come,' and he slammed the receiver down.

Jill accepted defeat and passed a wretched night, but next day after lunch she followed Luke out of the dining-room, and when he climbed the stairs to his flat she ran after him. The corridor was empty. As he fitted his key in the door she approached him nervously.

'Luke! Please, let me talk to you. It's ... very important.'

His mouth compressed, and he muttered something under his breath. Then he gave an ungracious shrug and stood aside to let her pass. 'All right, but cut it short. I'm due in theatre at two.'

She had worked out what she would say to him while she walked in the park. Now, faced with an angry and impatient Luke, her wits deserted her. 'I—I only wanted to apologise for that—that silly business over W-William.'

Luke flung himself in an armchair and closed his eyes, but he didn't ask her to sit down. 'And who told you about that? Gwyneth, of course. She would!'

'I—I know it sounded awful, what he said, but it w-wasn't exactly true.' She tried to explain her words in their correct context. 'It was a silly thing to say, but I—I lost my temper.'

Luke yawned and opened his eyes. 'Just why do you feel this urge to unburden yourself? I'm frankly not interested.'

They stared at one another, Jill unhappily, he with a disagreeable blend of boredom and contempt. 'You are interested!' Jill cried, 'or you wouldn't be so cross about it.'

'Correction, my dear girl, I am not interested in whom you do or don't fancy. I just wish you'd keep it to yourself. So if that's all . . .'

He rose to face her, his expression inimical, not one whit appeased by her apology. 'Luke, please believe——'

'Why do women never know when to shut up!' he exclaimed savagely, and stepped forward and pushed her against the wall. He held her pinned there, his hands on her shoulder, and his mouth was twisted into a mocking and unpleasant smile.

'So you'd prefer my kisses to William's? I'm flattered, Jill. And what would you do if I came to your bedroom tonight? Allow me to stay?'

'Stop it! Stop it!'

'Perhaps my original estimate was the true one,' he jeered. 'I put you down as a social climber, and then I thought I was mistaken. Now I'm not sure, though there's one way to find out.' When he kissed her Jill stayed passive, too shocked by his words to react. He ran his hands down her body and she responded at last, betrayed into momentary weakness.

'Oh, Luke,' she whispered, 'Luke!'

When he let her go her legs were trembling and her heart was pounding against her ribs. She leant against the wall and stared at him hopelessly, because it was obvious from his expression that his reaction had been quite different from hers.

'Well, well,' he said softly, 'perhaps William was right,' and then, with a despairing sob, Jill stumbled across the room and tore the door open.

She spent five minutes in her room, weeping wildly, face down on the bed. When the telephone rang she managed to answer it, but sounded so unlike herself that Jan Wyman asked, 'Jill? Aren't you well? You sound odd.'

'My nose is bunged up. I've got a cold,' Jill fibbed, and blew hard for good effect. She scrubbed at her eyes, while Jan told her that they were having trouble over tomorrow's list. One of Sir James' special instruments was away being repaired and they didn't have a spare.

'You'll be seeing him this afternoon, won't you? Could you break it to him gently?'

'Yes, of course, but he won't be very pleased about it.' By now Jill was outwardly composed, though inwardly a prey to humiliation and despair. She would have been far, far wiser to leave well alone. Luke had been annoyed with her before, but he would have got over it and forgiven her. Now it would be impossible for them to behave naturally together.

Meanwhile there was work do do, for however stormy her emotional life was, medicine came first. Jill ran a comb through her hair, washed her face and pulled on her white coat.

'Good grief, you do look out of sorts,' Bill observed, when she joined the rest of Sir James' team in Out-patients. Peter glanced at her briefly. Rumour had it that he was consoling himself—if consoling was the right word—with the blonde staff nurse on Jenner, so Gwyneth's nose for gossip had, as usual, been correct.

Sir James was petulant when he received Jan's message. 'How tiresome of Sister to send it just this week. I particularly wanted to do that case tomorrow. Perhaps if we rang the instrument makers...' He thawed out over tea, which he sometimes took in the residents' dining room.

'Conferring a great honour on us,' as Peter had said on another occasion. 'I trust you appreciate it, boys and girls?'

This afternoon Jill at least was grateful. Sir James monopolised the conversation, his rich voice booming out, so that even when Luke approached and sat at the lower end of the table, it was no more than a slight embarrassment. By keeping her eyes on her chief's face and listening attentively to the great man, Jill found she could behave quite normally. In time perhaps she would even feel normal inside.

That night she was called to Lister Ward by the staff nurse on duty. She sat in Sister's office, the patient's notes spread in front of her. The night nurse was a good girl, and had been quick to spot that there was something wrong with one of the post-operative patients. Jill had put her on antibiotics. She took out her pen and wrote a few words on the notes, and then the office door slid back and Luke's voice spoke from behind her.

'Hallo, Jill. Staff said you were in here.'

Jill held her breath for a few seconds, then she let out a long sigh, but didn't turn her head. Her hand clenched on the pen, and the other one gripped the table edge. The door shut with a little bang.

'I suppose you're absolutely furious with me,' Luke said quietly, 'and I really can't blame you. I behaved very badly yesterday. So I came to apologise.'

She muttered something inaudible.

'What was that?' he asked sharply, and then with the beginnings of exasperation, 'I didn't hear what you said.'

'I said,' Jill repeated, surprised at her own calmness, 'that we were quits now. We've both apologised.'

'What a stupid thing to say!' snapped Luke, losing his placatory manner with almost comical speed. 'I never met a girl who could put my back up quite so quickly.' He took her by the shoulder and shook her. Jill reacted with a speed that clearly surprised him, jumping to her feet and facing him, with a flushed and angry face.

'Don't touch me!'

'Oh, for God's sake!'

'Go away!'

He dug his hands in his pockets and glared down at her. 'What is it about you, Jill? I came here with the best of intentions, I swear I did.' He gave a short laugh. 'Though you'll have to take my word for it.'

To get rid of him, Jill said with freezing politeness that of course she believed him, and would he excuse her because she had work to do. It was plain from Luke's expression that he wasn't used to being dismissed in this summary fashion. He jerked the door open, and as he stepped through shot some final words at her.

'You needn't be afraid I shall make a pass at you again!' and he slammed the door with a bang that made the staff nurse hurry down the ward, to see what was going on.

At least Luke's attempt at an apology cleared the air between them; superficially they could meet without embarrassment, in dining-room or common-room, on ward rounds or in the operating theatre. Jill even assisted Luke in theatre one evening, when he was standing in for Peter for a few hours. Drinking tea afterwards in the surgeons' room, because she was determined to appear as normal as possible, Jill listened to the conversation between Luke and his anaesthetist.

'Peter not well?'

'No, he's fine, but he has some special date tonight. Meeting his girl-friend's family.' Luke spoke to the anaesthetist, but looked at Jill, a hint of speculation in his glance.

Jill tilted her head back defiantly and returned his stare. Luke smiled and the anaesthetist laughed. 'I say, that sounds as if he's hooked at last! Is he?'

'Who knows?' said Luke. 'Brothers are always the last to know,' and he went out to look for Jan, to ask her to join them.

The anaesthetist grinned at Jill. 'They're quite a pair, aren't they? Did you meet that American bird of Luke's?' and he whistled expressively.

When Luke came back with Jan, Jill was amused to realise that a romance seemed to be blossoming between the young Theatre Sister and the anaesthetic registrar. At least he was obviously very taken with her, and she certainly wasn't trying to discourage him. Luke watched them both benignly and removed Jill after a few minutes, on the excuse that he wanted to see a patient.

'Give them a little time on their own,' he observed rather surprisingly, for Luke was the last person Jill would have suspected of matchmaking. 'I like that girl,' he added, 'she's the best Sister at Queen's.'

'Do you think they're serious about each other?' Jill asked timidly, for Luke's temper these days was unpredictable. He rounded on her with a frown.

'*I* don't know. Ask Jan if you're so curious.'

Jan and her anaesthetist, thought Jill forlornly, Peter and his blonde. How lucky they were to have somebody special! Luke of course had Karen, and perhaps it was her absence that was making him so irritable.

'But she's coming back next week,' said Gwyneth, sharing a late supper on her own with Jill.

Jill pushed lukewarm macaroni cheese round her plate. 'How do you know?'

'Because I heard Luke telling Peter at breakfast. He was reading an air letter.'

'I suppose he was terribly excited?'

Gwyneth considered this and shook her head. 'Perhaps, but he didn't show it. Luke controls his feelings well.'

Maybe most of the time, thought Jill, but not with her. She made him lose his temper, and that was why he disliked her so much. But Karen made him laugh, and perhaps that, even more than her beauty, was what attracted Luke. He worked so hard and his job was so demanding, that off duty he needed to relax.

Jill had taken to slipping out for the odd hour, when she was free, and walking in the park. Previously she had joined in the endless games of cards that the residents played to while away the hours when they were on duty, but not working. Sometimes she stood in for Bill Mackie, so that he could slip home to see his wife and child, and he was only too pleased to do the same for her.

'Why this sudden yen for exercise?' he asked on one occasion.

'I don't know,' she admitted, 'I must be feeling restless.'

'Perhaps it's love,' Bill joked, caught the flicker of unhappiness on Jill's face and changed the subject quickly.

Now, walking by the lake in Regent's Park, head down and hands in her pockets, she came face to face with Luke and Karen, swinging along arm-in-arm.

Karen greeted her as an old friend. 'Hi, Jill! Isn't it a lovely day!'

It was one of those sunny days that February can produce, cold but with the promise of spring. Jill smiled and nodded and made to pass, but Karen was disposed to linger. Luke, after the slightest of nods, stood by and took no part in their conversation.

'Come on, Karen,' he said after a minute or two, 'I'm on call at three.' A sharp look for Jill. 'Surely you're not off duty today?'

'Bill's covering my patients for an hour.' At his frown she hastened on. 'I've been round the wards and there's absolutely nothing doing.'

'Just the same, I expect to be informed if you go out while you're on duty.'

'I wouldn't go out without someone covering.'

'Makes no difference. Don't do it again.'

'Oh, come on, honey! Do you have to be so stuffy?'

Luke's lips tightened. 'Please keep out of this, Karen. It's between Jill and me. You can walk back with us now.'

Making sure she did what she was told! Just for a second or two Jill nearly told him to go to hell, but he was strictly within his rights. As R.S.O. he was responsible for discipline among the residents, and if they didn't do their work properly he was the first person to reprimand them. Most of the senior staff knew that the residents took the odd hour off, and turned a blind eye as long as the patients didn't suffer. But not Luke, Jill thought bitterly, trudging resentfully along beside him. It would have to be he who had met her. Dear old Sir James wouldn't have minded, though Sir James probably never walked in the park.

'You've cast a blight over this nice day,' Karen reproved Luke, smiling winningly as she said it. Luke shrugged and the American girl winked at Jill. 'I sure am sorry for you, honey, having to put up with this man all the time. Is he always like this?'

'Only with me,' said Jill unwisely, and Luke's hand shot out. His fingers, digging into her arm, brought her to an abrupt halt. He looked so angry that Jill was glad of Karen's presence. At least she would put some sort of damper on his wrath.

'That's not true,' he said grimly, 'and you know it.'

She tugged vainly at her arm. 'Don't make a scene,' she begged. 'Not in front of Karen.'

His grip tightened painfully, and his face was tense with anger. Karen stared at them both in astonishment, but for once kept quiet.

'It's you who makes scenes, Jill, not me. If you'd obeyed the rules this wouldn't have happened.' He let her go and they walked along in a silence charged with emotion. Karen still looked puzzled, and glanced from one to the other of her companions several times, her smooth brow puckered in thought.

The American girl appeared at the residency quite often in the next few days. Sometimes she would wait for Luke in the common-room, chatting away to whoever happened to be there. Jill learnt that she was only over for a fortnight this time.

'So they're making the most of it,' observed Gwyneth. 'I wonder if they'll get engaged before she leaves.'

'I wonder how she'll take to living permanently in England,' someone else said, and Gwyneth shook her head.

'She'll probably talk him into emigrating. One more for the brain drain.'

'Hope she does,' said Bill, deadpan, 'more chance for us then!'

But Peter, arriving at that moment, expressed his opinion in no uncertain terms. 'Luke would never emigrate. If Karen wants him, she's the one who'll have to adapt.'

'Typical!' Gwyneth snorted. 'Absolutely typical!

The Haddons think they're the lords of creation, don't they?'

'Of course,' Peter said airily, 'because we are,' and then Karen came in and sat herself down by Jill, while Peter went off somewhere with Bill.

Karen waited until there was no one else around, and then asked if she was correct in thinking that Jill and Peter were no longer ... 'Well, you know...' Even Karen, who asked the most outrageous questions without giving offence, paused uncertainly.

Jill smiled at the other girl. 'It's all right, you're not upsetting me. Peter doesn't take me out any more.'

'I see.' Karen rested a hand lightly on Jill's. 'And you really don't mind, honey?'

Jill shook her head. 'It was never serious, though no one would believe it.'

'The old folk will be sorry. His grandparents. You were the one they rated high, not me.' Karen's tone was wry. 'They don't think I'm good enough for Luke, you know.'

'Oh, Karen, you must be imagining it!'

'Not on your life. They want someone intellectual, who talks their language. Like you,' said the American girl with remarkable lack of rancour. 'Oh, sure, they were too well-bred to say so, but I could tell,' and she managed a smile that didn't last.

What a nice girl she was, thought Jill. 'They'll come round, I'm sure. What matters is how Luke feels— and—and—there's not much doubt about that.'

'Isn't there?' Karen asked with a sigh. 'Would it surprise you to know that I make most of the running?' Jill stared and she went on quickly, 'He didn't ask me to come back. That was my idea. Mine! I'm not even sure he was pleased about it.' Perhaps she felt she had gone too far, for she jumped up from the sofa, blew her nose and started for the door. 'I must go do my face. Make myself beautiful for the wretched man!' and she was gone, leaving Jill to her thoughts.

Confused thoughts, and not especially happy ones. If Karen was right and Luke was not in love with her, there might still be hope. But hope for what? For an occasional date when he had nothing better to do? The odd chat when they met on the wards or in the common-room? There had been a girl house-surgeon, no longer at Q.C.H., who had been so infatuated with her registrar that she had made the poor man's life a misery. She had cruelly embarrassed him and made a laughing stock of herself. Jill vowed that she would never be like that. A girl should have more pride than to pursue a man who didn't want her. Not that she should need to tell herself that. If she had any self-respect at all, she wouldn't be in love with a man who behaved to her as Luke had done that day in the park. And on this salutary reflection she followed Karen out of the common-room.

CHAPTER TEN

SIR JAMES MACAULAY sometimes invited other eminent surgeons to take his Tuesday morning teaching round. These occasions were usually advertised in advance, but either he had forgotten to tell his juniors, or Jill hadn't been around when he did, that Professor Haddon was going to honour them with his presence. 'Honour' was the word, for the old man's prestige was enormous. The entrance hall was packed and there was an air of expectancy in the gathering when she arrived.

Jill made her way to Bill's side. 'What's up? Are we expecting Royalty?'

'Almost,' said Bill, 'the great Prof. Haddon in person. Surely you knew?'

'No, I didn't.' There was no time for more, because the head porter swung the heavy doors open and Sir James marched in, to beam on his assembled juniors with obvious pleasure at the large turnout. Professor Haddon wasn't given to beaming. He cast a surprised look round and made some dry remark to his companion, and Sir James, chuckling, led him to the lift. In the lift Jill was squashed into a corner between Bill and Peter, but Professor Haddon saw her when they came out, and greeted her with unexpected warmth.

Sir James drew her into the little group about the Professor, and she ended up in the ward standing close beside him.

'Whose patient is this?' asked Sir James, and Jill, who preferred to be out of the limelight, stepped back as Bill moved forward.

'That was my toe you trod on,' Luke said under his breath, thereby spoiling her concentration and causing her to miss half the great man's words. At the next bed she stood as far away from Luke as she could, and received a sardonic look that told her he knew what she was up to.

'That was absolutely great,' enthused Gwyneth, who had played truant from a medical round so as not to miss the occasion. 'He's the most stimulating teacher I've ever heard. Now I know where Luke gets it from. Good lord, the old man's surely not going to eat here!' for Professor Haddon, accompanied by his elder grandson, had just entered the dining-room.

He stood in the doorway, a tall commanding figure, erect in spite of his age, while Luke crossed the room to Jill's table. 'You dashed off so fast at the end of the round that I didn't have a chance to speak to you. My grandfather wants you to lunch with us.'

'That's very—very kind of him,' Jill stammered, 'b-but I've already ordered.'

The maid placed two plates of curry in front of Gwyneth and her. Gwyneth shuddered, and gave Luke a cheeky smile. 'Take her away, Mr Haddon, and save her from food poisoning!'

'But I don't think——'

'Bill will eat yours,' Luke said firmly, removing Jill's plate and handing it to the Scotsman. 'Grandpa will be most disappointed if you don't come.'

To refuse would be churlish, and besides, Jill wanted to go. 'I'll just fetch a coat,' she said as she went past Professor Haddon, and smiled to herself as Luke shouted up the stairs after her, 'Hurry up! We're starving. Meet you at the main entrance.'

Thank goodness she had gone to her room before lunch, so that she didn't have to spend any time on her appearance. She snatched up a coat and ran downstairs again, to find Mrs Haddon in the hall with the two men. A delightful surprise, and something of a relief, because lunch with the Professor and Luke on their own might have been quite an ordeal. They went by taxi to a small restaurant in Soho, whose proprietor was the grandson of the original owner.

'I used to come here as a medical student,' Professor Haddon told Jill, 'and I wanted to see what it's like now.'

It was smarter than it had been in his day, he decided, but the food was still excellent.

Mrs Haddon was charming to Jill and made it plain that she would welcome another visit from the girl.

'I've already told you, Grandma,' Luke said with a touch of dryness, 'if Peter brings a girl down, it won't be Jill.'

Mrs Haddon sighed. 'Must you be so—so tactless, Luke?'

'Jill doesn't mind. Do you, little one?'

'Would it make any difference if I did?' Jill retorted with spirit, and the Professor chuckled.

'That's right, my dear. Stand up to him.'

Mrs Haddon was not to be deflected, and asked Jill when she had another free weekend. 'Then could you spend the Sunday with us? You are free? Good.' She suggested that Jill should come down on the ten o'clock train and travel back with Luke in the evening. Dismayed, Jill waited for Luke to offer some objection, but smiling pleasantly at her (and with a touch of malice?), he assured his grandmother that nothing would give him greater pleasure. Lunch over, they took a taxi back to Queen's, and after depositing Luke and Jill the old people went on to the station.

'Half a day in London is as much as they care for,' Luke remarked, 'they're far happier in the country.'

That gave her an opening. 'About my visit——'

Luke held up a hand. 'Nothing to discuss, my dear girl. It's all arranged.'

'Will Karen be there?'

'She's gone back to America.'

'Peter?'

'I doubt it. Don't worry, Jill, it'll be a nice cosy day! Just you and me and the grandparents.' But the look he gave her was about as cosy as a tiger's before he leaps on his prey. Luke, she thought uneasily, was getting a good deal of amusement out of his grandmother's invitation, and she didn't know why. If she really wanted to get out of the visit she would have to think up some excuse, but though common sense told her it was unwise to go, her heart urged her to accept the chance, and make the most of it.

On Sunday week the weather was perfect, brilliantly sunny but with a lingering frost on the fields. When the train ran into the little country station her heart began the all too familiar pounding, and she schooled her face to careful composure. Her 'Hallo' was perhaps too off-hand, for Luke stared at her hard and the corners of his mouth quirked.

'This one of your off days?' he inquired as they walked to the car.

'I'm sorry?'

'Off days. We all have them—you rather more than most.' He shut the car door on her and strolled round to his side. As he slid in beside her his smile grew. 'Well?'

'Well what?' she asked feebly, because his proximity robbed her of logical thought.

'Funny girl!' he exclaimed. 'I wish I understood you better.' The smile was charming now and scattered her wits still further. He laid his hand on hers and she nearly jumped out of her seat. 'Don't spoil Grandma's day, Jill. She's looking forward to your visit.'

'What an odd thing to say. I'm looking forward to it too.'

'Liar,' he said pleasantly, and started the car. 'At least, you might have enjoyed it if I hadn't been here, But anyway, for Grandma's sake, shall we call a truce?'

'I can't think why you wanted me to come if you feel we're on such bad terms.' Her voice had sharpened and risen in pitch. Careful, she thought, she mustn't get involved in a sparring match, because Luke always won.

He laughed. 'If you remember, it was entirely Grandma's idea, but actually I've been looking forward to your visit.'

'Really?' she managed, her tone disbelieving.

'You lend a little spice to life! I like my girls with a bit of spirit.'

He said it casually, half as a joke. *My girls*, indeed! She wasn't one of his girls, and never would be. If she couldn't be *the* girl she wasn't prepared to act as a stand-in until Karen returned. Jill stared out of the window at the gentle Sussex countryside, and wondered if she'd reacted more than his remark warranted. She didn't think so, for Luke's behaviour today was subtly different. He behaved as if he was more aware of her as a woman. His eyes had travelled over her appreciatively when she stepped off the train. His smile had held genuine warmth when he greeted her.

She must not, she decided, spend any time alone with him today. If he was bored, and disposed to flirt with her because she was available, she couldn't trust her response. She might lose her head and give herself away. Some girls could indulge in casual lovemaking and emerge unscathed, but Jill knew that she wasn't one of them.

After lunch, to her relief, they all went out for a walk together, through the woods that grew down to the edge of the garden. The wind had risen and the trees swayed, till the whole world was filled with a great rushing sound. Exhilarated by sun and air, and safe in the Haddons' company, Jill danced along joyfully, drawing smiles from Luke's grandparents. They were darlings and she loved them. She imagined for a few foolish moments what it would be like if Luke fell in love with her. 'They'd be pleased,' she thought, 'I know they would,' and then reality returned with Luke's dry voice, telling her to stop dashing ahead, they were turning back.

'No need for you to return,' said Mrs Haddon, 'you and Jill go on.'

Jill started to say that they might as well all go back together, but Luke took firm hold of her arm and walked her on. 'See you later,' he called to his grandparents, and marched her down a side path. It led into a small clearing where primroses grew. Jill was oppressed by his closeness, and by her consciousness of their isolation in this lonely spot. She withdrew her arm carefully and said she wanted to pick primroses, 'For my room at Q.C.H.'

She knelt on the ground and began plucking them, while Luke leant against a tree trunk. She sensed that he was watching her, but avoided looking at him. He sang softly under his breath, some old English folk tune, and his voice was rich and true. Deliberately she moved away from him, picking as she went, clumsier than usual because he was there. When he came after her she didn't hear him, and gasped as he stooped to draw her to her feet.

'Stop play-acting, Jill. You don't want to pick primroses.' His hands slid down her arms, tightened and drew her towards him. She shut her eyes, because she couldn't bear to look at him. 'You want this as much as I do,' said Luke, his voice suddenly harsh, and he kissed her fiercely. When she responded he became more gentle, stroking her hair and murmuring endearments that meant nothing, she told herself forlornly as she clung on to the last shreds of common sense.

He was missing Karen and he wanted to console himself with another girl, and because of her response that day in his room, he expected her to be willing.

'Let me go!' she cried, and gave a furious push that took him by surprise. She retreated across the clearing, but he didn't come after her. 'You've got a nerve!' Her voice sounded shrill and unattractive, and with an effort she lowered it. 'You're the most conceited man I've ever met! I should have thought you'd have known how I feel about you, after all this time.'

If she had hoped to discomfit him she should have known better. 'Not conceited,' Luke said quietly, 'and I know exactly how you feel about me.' At her protesting gasp his eyes narrowed and he crossed to her side, crushing the primroses she had dropped a few minutes earlier. 'Physical attraction has nothing to do with liking, little one.' He smiled with his mouth but not with his eyes. 'You resent me because I attract you, though you're not honest enough to admit it. I've known what was wrong between us since the first time we met.'

'How could you?'

'Because I feel the same way,' Luke said very quietly. 'Don't worry, I shan't touch you again.' He started walking back to the main path and she followed unhappily, regretting now her words of rejection. He hadn't pretended to be in love with her, but if he was attracted to her it was a start. He might have come to love her—and then she remembered Karen and gave a despairing sigh.

'What was that sigh for?' Luke asked levelly.

'You're ... angry with me, aren't you?' She answered his question with another.

'And that makes you sigh?' Luke asked with open disbelief. 'I rather thought you were getting a kick out of the situation.' He walked so fast that she had to run to catch up with him. 'Of course I'm not. I—I hate quarrelling with you.'

'Do you indeed?' The disbelief was still there. 'Then you shouldn't be so provocative.' He stopped suddenly and swung round on her, his eyes accusing. 'I hate girls who lead men on, then act outraged at the result.'

Jill's mouth opened, but for a few seconds no words came. When she finally spoke it was with mounting anger. 'You think I wanted you to kiss me? You know quite well that I suggested going back to the house with your grandparents. I didn't choose to be alone with you. I knew what would happen if I was.' Her voice trembled and she gulped miserably. 'This is s-stupid. You're so—so unreasonable.'

He started walking again. 'All right, Jill, I'm sorry. Perhaps I misjudged you. I suppose I thought you were more sophisticated than you really are.'

'When men say sophisticated they mean willing,' Jill snapped, and he laughed.

'Point taken. I won't make the same mistake again.' He rubbed a hand over his eyes as if he was tired. 'Do you think we could put on a façade of friendliness for Grandma's sake? I'll think of an excuse to leave early.'

Heavy-hearted, Jill agreed that they could at least be civilised, and they walked the rest of the way in silence. He was right, of course. She wasn't sophisticated when it came to sexual behaviour. She wanted love from him, and that he couldn't offer, and he was too honest to pretend what he didn't feel.

They left early, because Luke said that he wanted to look round the wards before morning. His grandmother, disappointed, said that they must come again soon. 'Odd, isn't it,' observed Luke, as they drove through the main gates, 'how Grandma's mind works? She thinks she's well on the way to a bit of successful matchmaking,' and he laughed derisively.

'Shows what good actors we are,' Jill retorted. 'Please, Luke, couldn't we just forget about today? I know I want to,' and again there was that humiliating tremble in her voice.

He raised a hand from the wheel in an impatient

gesture. 'Don't get worked up again. I'm not in the mood for another scene,' and for the second time he rubbed his eyes.

'Headache?' Jill asked, and he nodded.

'Keep getting them—I really must have my eyes tested.'

She was filled with remorse when she saw how strained he was looking. He had earned a weekend's relaxation, and today had been ruined for him. She longed to tell him to stop the car somewhere, to take him in her arms and stroke his forehead. The longing was painful in its intensity because she loved him so much, but all she said was, 'Shall I drive for a bit?'

'Good lord, no! It's not that bad.' He sounded staggered at the suggestion, for Luke was not a man who liked admitting to any weakness.

They scarcely spoke for the rest of the journey, and when they reached the hospital Luke climbed out of the car stiffly. They walked into the residency together. 'You don't really have to go round the wards?' Jill asked, and he shook his head, smiling faintly.

'Just a smokescreen for Grandma. Goodnight, Jill.'

'Goodnight.' She watched his tall figure, walking less vigorously than usual, until he turned the corner towards the stairs. He was either tired, or his headache was worse than he was prepared to admit. Or he was feeling thoroughly fed up. Perhaps a bit of all three, exacerbated by her behaviour and Karen's absence. She thought, as she had often done before, that Karen couldn't be truly in love with Luke, to consider him so little. She had no job to which she was compelled to return. If she had really loved him she would have stayed with him, and not expected to be taken out every night. Just to be with him should have been enough, as it certainly would have been for Jill.

Then she remembered Karen's words about being the one who made the running, and wondered if the American girl was changing her tactics. Perhaps she hoped that if she stayed in California Luke would follow her out there?

Jill opened the door of her room and had a sudden thought. Luke could do with some aspirin, however much he despised the homely remedy. She took the bottle off the shelf above her washbasin, and went quickly down to his flat before her courage deserted her. She knocked on his door and waited nervously for his 'Come in.'

He was lying back in one of the armchairs, and she was certainly the last person he was expecting.

'I brought you some aspirin.' She shook a couple into her palm, filled a glass with water and put them into his hand. He took them with surprising meekness, which told her more about his condition than any words could have done.

'Thanks, Jill. It was kind of you to bother.'

'No bother. It's cold in here. Shall I light your fire?' She guessed that he was feeling too flaked out to make even that small effort. She went down on her knees to put a match to the fire, and Luke watched her through half-closed eyes.

'Heaping coals of fire on my head, as they say?'

She jumped to her feet. 'Just being friendly. I hope your headache soon goes.'

She had her hand on the door when he spoke again. 'Stay a few minutes.'

Politeness? He couldn't really want her. 'You'd do better going straight to bed,' Jill said firmly, and went back to her room, feeling a little less unhappy than she had been before.

'When do you finish on my firm, Miss Bentley?' asked Sir James one afternoon, when Out-patients was over.

'At the end of the month,' Jill said, and something about her tone made her chief look at her thoughtfully.

'Walk to my car with me, Jill.' When his mood was

benign he called them by their first names. As he paced along he asked her if she had any plans for the future.

Leaving Q.C.H. meant leaving Luke, with the only chance of seeing him if she made the occasional return visit. Everyone assumed that Luke was bound to get the Senior Registrar's post, which was coming up for interview in a fortnight's time.

'I haven't any plans,' Jill said with a sigh.

'Then don't you think it's time you made some?' Sir James sounded almost severe.

'I suppose so.'

Frowning at her vagueness, he told her that a post would be coming up at the end of April, at a hospital fifteen miles rom London. 'I go there once a week, and share a house surgeon with another man. It's not Q.C.H., of course, but it's a busy hospital in a growing industrial town. Think about it and let me know soon.'

'It's very kind of you, Sir James, but I'm not sure I want to do another surgical job. I had thought of obstetrics next.' Sir James' mouth pursed, for he expected his favours to be received with more enthusiasm. 'I—I expect I'll be going into general practice,' Jill rushed on, anxious not to offend the great man, whose reference she might need in the future, 'so I'll have to do obstetrics.'

The surgeon thawed, and patted her hand. 'Plenty of time for that. You're very young, my dear. Let me know what you decide.'

After two jobs at Q.C.H. she certainly couldn't expect another one, but a second surgical post would be merely marking time. 'What would you do?' Jill asked Gwyneth, and Gwyneth said, 'Ask Peter.'

'Why Peter?'

'Well . . . he knows the ropes,' said Gwyneth vaguely, and at the end of supper she waved at Peter as he was leaving the dining-room. He came over to their table and the Welsh girl asked his opinion on Jill's problem. 'She doesn't really want the job, but she's reluctant to offend the old man.'

Peter said airily that it would do the old fool good if someone turned him down, and Gwyneth looked exasperated. 'All very well for you to talk, you've got it made. But we don't all have famous relations.'

Peter blinked at the sharpness of her tone, but he sat down and seemed to be thinking more seriously about Jill's affairs. 'Thing is,' he said slowly, 'is there any point in her doing another six months' surgery?'

Luke tapped him on the shoulder. 'Coming? I want to see that patient of yours before I go out.'

'Just a moment,' said Peter, 'Jill has a problem,' and he told his brother what it was.

Jill could have done without all this attention. She said awkwardly that they couldn't possibly be interested, but Luke's face was serious as he answered her. 'Of course we're interested. It's important not to make the wrong decision. I agree with Peter that you'd be wasting time doing another surgical job. One's enough unless you're planning to specialise. Look for something in obstetrics or paediatrics.'

She had told him in the past that she intended going into practice, or just possibly anaesthetics. He asked her if she had quite given up the latter idea, and raised his eyebrows at her hesitant reply. 'You mustn't let yourself drift, my girl,' he said severely. 'Set your sights on something definite and aim straight for it.'

As he was doing, but Luke was a man and ambitious, and she was a girl, whose emotions were playing havoc with her common sense. Off duty at any rate, for when she was working she was too dedicated a doctor to allow her thoughts to wander. After a weekend of brooding on the problems she was no nearer a solution, but knew she must make up her mind, for Sir

James had an excellent memory and would certainly ask what she had decided. On Monday evening she telephoned her father, and Dr Bentley came down on the same side as Luke. He urged her to have a good holiday, and then apply for some post that would be useful when she went into general practice.

'The summer's coming,' he pointed out. 'Why don't you look for something in the West Country?' Six months by the sea did appeal, for Jill loved swimming and was a keen sailor. She agreed that it was a good idea, and promised to come home when she finished at Q.C.H. So next day she gave Sir James his answer, a little apologetically, and expecting a cool reply. He heard her out and was pleasanter than she had expected. Perhaps she had been worrying unnecessarily, for in Sir James' scheme of things a house surgeon was not of much consequence.

'A pity, my dear. I should have been pleased to have you for another six months, but I expect you've made a wise decision. Yes, I'm sure you have.'

The trouble was that she hadn't really made any decision except a negative one, but the effort of applying for jobs seemed beyond her in her present mood ... she had three weeks more with Sir James and then she would be leaving. Luke came up to her one day on the ward, and asked her what she had lined up for the future. When she said nothing, he frowned and said he couldn't understand her. Why not get on with it?

'I'm having a holiday before I make any plans.'

He looked scornful. 'So all right, you need a holiday, but apply for some jobs now or you'll have a longer holiday than you want—or need!'

What he said was true, for all good posts had many applicants, and she might have to apply for quite a few before she was lucky. 'Yes, I know,' she agreed, 'but I can always fill in doing locums.'

As he was doing, but he still looked disapproving. 'I

don't understand you, Jill. Unless you're careful you'll become a drifter, going from one dead-end job to another.'

'No, I shan't. I'm tired just now, and not in the mood for making decisions, but when I've had a holiday it'll be different.'

'You hope!' he said sardonically, and left her with evident displeasure. Jill wondered why he wasted his time pointing out the error of her ways. He had scarcely spoken to her since that disastrous Sunday in Sussex. Peter too, beyond formal politeness, had shown no interest in her. The Haddon brothers, Jill thought wryly, had written her off. She was glad now that her present appointment was all but finished. Once just seeing Luke had been better than nothing; now seeing him in the distance, or exchanging the occasional word about a surgical problem, was worse than not seeing him at all.

She longed to feel his arms round her again and wept for her lost opportunities, but saw no way in which she could put the clock back, without loss of self-respect. She had never chased a man in her life and she was not going to do it now. Besides, she had a shrewd idea that her attraction for Luke had been of the slightest, and based more on the fact that she was there than on any stronger force. He couldn't be interested in her or he would have asked her out again. He was not, after all, engaged to Karen—or so said Gwyneth, who had it from Peter's current girl-friend, the blonde on Jenner.

'Peter says they parted on bad terms, though he doesn't know why. Could be Luke asked her to stay and she wasn't prepared to.'

'Or she wanted him to find a job in the States and *he* wasn't prepared to,' said Jill, with a fine show of indifference. 'It's their affair, isn't it?' and she walked off, leaving Gwyneth staring after her.

CHAPTER ELEVEN

IT was Bill Mackie who told Jill about Luke's appointment. He had won the coveted post of Senior Registrar on the surgical unit against stiff opposition. 'Though I suppose there was never much doubt about it!'

'Not much,' Jill agreed, and wondered if she should seek out Luke to congratulate him. It was after all a major step up in his career. Better not, she decided, for her good wishes would mean nothing to him, and the less she had to do with him, the safer it would be, for she was afraid of breaking down and making a fool of herself. In fact she was relieved, when it came to the night of her farewell party, to find that he was first on call, and occupied all evening in the operating theatre. Peter looked in, but spent most of the time in a corner with his staff nurse.

The old patterns were changing, Jill reflected sadly. The first year after qualification they had retained a good deal of their old student light-heartedness. The junior residents at Q.C.H. all knew each other very well, for they had been through five years at medical school together. Now they were splitting up, apart from the lucky few who were staying on in other jobs. They were growing up, thought Jill, and felt a pang for the carefree life that would never come again.

She tried to explain this when Gwyneth and Bill joined her, and Bill asked why she was looking so broody. 'Nostalgia for the past, it's called,' nodded Gwyneth, 'we all have it sometimes,' and Bill said drily that married men didn't have time for these fancies. They were too busy trying to make ends meet.

Jill saw Luke briefly next day, at breakfast. She came in late and sat facing him, because there was no other chair vacant. She was careful to avoid looking in his direction, though when there was a general movement at the registrars' table, she looked up involuntarily. He was leaving with several others. He passed within a few feet of her, glanced her way, paused for a moment and said something to Peter. Peter nodded and went on, waving a casual hand in her direction, for he had already said goodbye to her last night.

Luke strolled over and rested one hand on the back of Bill's chair. 'So you're off today, Jill? All the best for the future.'

The pain was worse than she had expected, but mercifully his farewell was brief. 'Look us up some time,' Luke went on, nodded and walked off. Jill swallowed painfully on the lump in her throat and tried to pour herself another cup of coffee, but her hand shook so much that she couldn't do it.

'Let me,' Bill said quietly, and took the pot from her hand. He looked at her with compassion. Kind, stolid Bill, who noticed more than most people. All around them the usual animated conversations went on, about medicine and politics, girl-friends, cars. No one else, Jill thought thankfully, had noticed her reaction to Luke's casual farewell, and after today there would be no more need to pretend she didn't care.

April in South Devon could be a beautiful month, and this one was no exception. The weather was kind for Jill's holiday, and the lovely burgeoning countryside balm to her unhappy spirit. She grew, if not content, at least resigned. Hundreds, thousands of girls, had unhappy love affairs, and got over them, led useful lives, married someone else.

If her family noticed that she was quieter than usual they didn't comment on it. Marcia, rather surprisingly, echoed Dr Bentley's hope that she would spend the entire holiday with them, and even Betty was more agreeable than usual, but then she had a new young man in tow, and was hardly ever at home. So much for her brief infatuation for Luke, thought Jill, and envied her little sister's superficial nature.

One afternoon her father came back from a clinical meeting at their local general hospital. He told Jill that there was an unexpected vacancy in the anaesthetic department. The newly appointed resident anaesthetist had let the hospital down badly. Only five days before he was due to start at St Mary's, he had written to inform them that he had accepted another post.

'A sign of the times,' Marcia said cynically. 'Young people aren't reliable these days.'

'Doctors should be,' her husband said gravely. 'He's left them badly in the lurch.' He turned to Jill and asked if she would be interested. 'I've told them you're free and they would be very grateful for your help.'

'But I've had no experience in anaesthetics,' she objected, 'just a few sessions as a student.'

'Everyone's the same to begin with. A junior anaesthetist is always supervised.'

'I'll ... think about it.'

'Harold Dalton would be your chief,' her father said persuasively, 'I'm sure you'd enjoy working for him.'

She had known Dr Dalton all her life, had been at school with his daughter, and was on nodding terms with nearly all the senior staff at St Mary's. It would be less lonely working in her home town, and loneliness was something to be avoided until she had got over Luke.

'I'll go and see them tomorrow,' she promised, and her father looked pleased. Now that Marcia and Jill were getting on better he seemed to enjoy his elder daughter's company more than he had done in the past.

Jill went to St Mary's the following morning, had coffee with Dr Dalton and another anaesthetist, and was talked into accepting the vacancy. Her suggestion that she might do a locum until they found someone more experienced was quickly demolished.

'We'd have to advertise and interview all over again, and that would take weeks,' Dr Dalton pointed out.

'By which time you'd no longer be inexperienced,' added the younger anaesthetist, a pleasant man called Dr Green.

So she signed a contract in the secretary's office and agreed to start work in two days' time. Over the weekend she rang Gwyneth up to tell her about the new job. Gwyneth congratulated her, then told her all the latest gossip. Right at the end she threw in the information that Peter had got engaged to his blonde.

'Surprising, isn't it? I thought Peter wasn't the marrying kind, though I suppose an engagement can always be broken. You ... don't mind, do you, Jill? You really don't mind?'

Jill felt the old familiar irritation that even Gwyneth should need to ask that question. 'I'm delighted for them,' she said quickly. 'When are they going to get married?'

Gwyneth was vague about that. 'I expect they'll get around to it some time.' She sounded as if she was about to end the conversation, so Jill said carefully, 'And Luke?' She was amazed at how normally it came out. Gwyneth seemed to find nothing odd in the question.

She laughed and said that he was like a bear with a sore head. 'Worse than usual, so think yourself lucky to be away from here. Peter says it's because Karen and he have split up. Jill? Oh, I thought you'd rung off.'

Jill said slowly, 'No, no, I was just ... thinking. I really meant what does Luke think about Peter's engagement?'

Gwyneth chuckled. 'Probably thinks it's high time he made an honest woman of her. As a matter of fact I think he's rather pleased, from something I overheard him saying to one of the other registrars.'

Gwyneth was a great one for overhearing interesting conversations. 'Pleased it's her and not me, probably,' Jill said with a trace of bitterness.

After Gwyneth had rung off she sat by the telephone, staring out unseeingly at the cliffs and the sea beyond, for their house was built on a headland overlooking the town. Usually she enjoyed the view, but after Gwyneth's news she was lost in thoughts of Luke, wondering if he was very unhappy. If only she had still been at Queen's he might have turned to her for consolation; or to any one of a dozen other girls, common sense told her, for Luke was attractive and much sought after.

The new job was taxing but interesting. The anaesthetists, true to their word, gave her all the guidance she needed, and by the following weekend she was already beginning to acquire confidence.

'You're a born anaesthetist,' smiled Dr Green, at the end of the Friday afternoon orthopaedic session. 'Quick to learn, and quiet.'

'Quietness being the quality that matters,' observed the orthopaedic surgeon, nodding companionably at Jill. 'A good anaesthetist is one who doesn't chatter.'

'We leave that to the surgeon,' joked Dr Green, winking at Jill.

They couldn't have been nicer to her. There were even times when she was able to put Luke out of her mind, though not for long, and when she did think about him the pain was as sharp, the despair as acute.

Dr Green told her that they were on together for the weekend. 'But I shan't leave you on your own, I promise, until you've had more experience.'

If Friday night was anything to go by she was going to acquire experience very quickly. They had four emergencies and went to bed at three. Jill slept late, because she had no routine work on Saturday morning, and arrived in the hospital dining-room to the remains of breakfast. She assured the maid that a cup of coffee was all she wanted, and took it into the window embrasure, where the early spring sunshine was surprisingly warm.

St Mary's Hospital was built on the opposite headland to the one where her home was. Still a little sleepy after her disturbed night, Jill sat and watched the sparkle on the sea and the white horses pounding into the shore. She felt lazy, reluctant to move. Then the telephone rang and she rose to answer it.

'Dr Bentley? There's someone to see you. Shall I send him up?'

'Who is it?' Jill asked, but the switchboard operator seemed to be carrying on several conversations at once. 'Hallo? Hallo?' Exasperated, she put the receiver down, wondering if her father had called in to see how she was doing. She opened the door and heard someone running up the stairs. Not her father, then, since he was past the age for such energetic behaviour. Round the bend in the stairs came a man, and Jill's hand tightened on the doorknob. She stared in disbelief, and then he had reached the landing and was looking round impatiently, saw her and walked quickly down the corridor.

'Luke!' It was the merest whisper. She was incapable of more.

He looked over her shoulder into the empty dining-room, took her by the arm and drew her in, shutting the door after them. He leant against the door, smiling at her rather uncertainly, as if he wasn't sure of his welcome.

'Surprised, Jill? I suppose I should have let you know I was coming.'

'It ... was unexpected,' she managed in a curiously croaky little voice. 'What are you doing here, Luke?'

'What do you think?' he asked quietly. They were standing close together, so that he only had to reach out to take her in his arms. When he kissed her she clung to him, and everything else was blotted out in the joy of their lovemaking. Someone tried to open the door, but Luke was leaning against it.

'It's stuck,' came a surprised voice from outside, then another push.

'Hell!' said Luke softly, and let her go. She backed away from him, flushed and dishevelled, and he jerked the door open crossly. A couple of maids stood outside, a trolley between them, their curiosity open as they looked from Luke to Jill.

'Sorry, sir, we didn't know anyone was still here.' The maids bustled in and began to clear the tables. To the accompaniment of clattering crockery Luke took Jill's arm.

'Can we go to your room? Have you time?'

He kept his hand on her arm as if he was reluctant to let her go. When they reached her room he drew her towards him again. 'Oh, Jill, I've missed you so much! I don't think I slept at all last night, wondering whether you'd be pleased to see me.'

At that she flung her arms round his neck and turned up her face to his, and only when they were more in control of themselves did she start to ask questions. 'Why didn't you tell me you were coming? How did you know where I was? Did you *really* miss me?'

He answered the last question first. 'I missed you all right, my love. I couldn't sleep by night and I couldn't work by day.' He amended that with a rather twisted smile. 'Well, I worked, of course, but I found it difficult to concentrate. You're the only girl who's ever distracted me like that, but then you're the only girl I've ever loved.'

She was sitting on his knee, in the one easy chair the

room contained, and when he said this she laid her head against his shoulder, because she didn't want to look at him as she asked the next question.

'But ... Karen?'

Luke shifted in the chair and tipped her head back, so that he could look into her eyes. 'Karen's a great girl, but not for me.'

'We all thought——'

'I know exactly what everyone thought.'

'But you saw so much of her. Weren't you even a little in love with her? Gwyneth said you were unhappy because you'd parted from her.'

'Gwyneth doesn't know everything,' Luke said crisply. 'It was your absence I was unhappy about, not Karen's.' He put his hands on either side of her face and kissed her with passion. 'No, Jill, I was not even a little in love with Karen, nor she with me. I was repaying hospitality for the fabulous time they gave me in California. Satisfied?'

She nodded, but spared a thought for the American girl, who had been fonder of Luke than he had ever realised. There was a knock on the door and Jill jumped to her feet, smoothing back her hair. It was another maid, asking if she could make the bed. Luke sighed and rose too.

'Is there anywhere in this damn place where we can have some privacy?' he grumbled, and Jill gave his hand a squeeze as they walked down the corridor.

She pointed out that she was on duty, so couldn't leave the hospital, but suggested that he go for a stroll round the harbour and come back at eleven for coffee. It was only after he had gone that she realised she hadn't asked him how long he was staying.

She spent some time in the wards looking at last night's emergency patients, then there was a new admission to see, a young boy for appendectomy. By the time she arrived in the dining-room Luke was already there, sitting with Dr Green and the surgeon on call. They all turned as she came in, and Luke pulled up a chair for her by his side.

'Your friend picked a bad weekend to come down,' the surgeon observed. 'I'm afraid the work's piling up already.'

'Can't be helped,' said Luke, 'it was still worth coming,' and the smile he gave Jill made her heart beat faster.

She looked at him with such radiant happiness that their two colleagues exchanged amused glances, and excused themselves shortly afterwards. Luke laid his hand over hers. 'Decent types. Tactful, too.' He told her that he had booked a room for the night at a hotel on the waterfront, and that he would travel back to London on Sunday night, by sleeper, as he had come down. That he hadn't telephoned her beforehand because he had been uncertain of his reception.

That was the moment when two of the residents came in for coffee, and Luke muttered something very rude under his breath. 'It is their dining-room after all,' Jill pointed out, then looked at her watch and said it was time for the appendectomy.

Luke said that he would wait for her in her room, and added with a grin, 'Twenty minutes for an appendectomy! I'll see you at twelve,' but it was nearer twelve-thirty before they were out of theatre.

The afternoon was blessedly quiet, so Jill brought their tea upstairs, and they had a couple of hours to themselves. She sat on the floor by the fire, leaning back against Luke's chair. It was then that she asked him the most important question of all.

'Was it only after I'd gone that you knew you loved me?'

She had turned to look at him and he stared back at her, his expression serious. 'I fell in love with you a long time ago.'

'But you were always so horrid! Well, nearly always. Just occasionally you were nice.'

'That was when my guard was down,' he said drily, and at her questioning look, 'You were Peter's girl, my love. I tried very hard to dislike you, because I was afraid of liking you too much.'

'But I kept telling you——'

'It wasn't only a question of what *you* felt about Peter. I thought *he* cared about you. I thought so right up to the day he got himself engaged. For all I know he did that on the rebound!'

Jill was distressed by this idea. 'Oh, no! She's such a nice girl, and he was interested in her before——' She broke off, colouring.

'Before you came along,' Luke finished a trifle sternly. 'I don't think you have any idea what you do to a man, sweetheart. That aloof air is more provocative than you realise. It certainly had Peter thoroughly confused,' and he laughed and ruffled her hair.

'I'm not aloof,' Jill murmured, 'I've always been a bit shy.'

'After five years of medical school?' he teased, and slid his hand down to the nape of her neck. Her breath came more quickly. She moved away from him.

'If you do that I can't think straight.'

'I don't see the need for thinking right now,' he murmured, and slipped down beside her on the rug.

'Please, Luke, I'm on duty. The housemen often came in——'

'Do they, indeed! Just see to it they don't get ideas!' He moved back to the chair and rested his hands on his knees, chin cupped, eyes amused. 'Since love-making is out, we'd better make conversation!'

He told her that the week since he had heard about Peter's engagement had seemed the longest one in his life. He hadn't been free until Friday night, and he hadn't wanted to write or telephone. But he had telephoned his grandmother, because he had to talk to someone. She had listened with sympathy, told him he had been behaving very foolishly, and urged him to go down to Devon at the first opportunity.

'Do you know what the old lady said?' Luke's smile was a little wry. 'That Grandpa and she knew right from the beginning that you would never marry Peter. That we were attracted to each other the first time we met!'

'I thought you were horrid!' Jill protested.

'And I thought you were beautiful! So Grandma did a bit of matchmaking. Remember that last time she invited you down?'

They smiled at each other a little ruefully. 'I thought I was just a substitute for Karen,' said Jill. 'A girl has some pride.'

'And I was still feeling guilty about Peter, until things got out of hand.' He took a handful of her hair and tugged it gently. 'What a lot of time we've wasted! How soon does this locum of yours finish?'

When she told him that she had signed on for six months he frowned, then his face relaxed. 'That's no problem. You're entitled to leave after a month's notice.'

'It seems rather mean,' she demurred.

Luke was used to having his own way and could be very persuasive, especially when he took her in his arms and said he was damned if he was waiting until autumn. He wanted to marry her now. 'There's a flat near Queen's that would suit us perfectly. Goes with the job if I want it. Hand in your notice on Monday, darling, and we'll get married as soon as you finish.'

A little unhappily, because she loved him so much and wanted to please him, Jill said that of course she would talk to the anaesthetists on Monday. But she wasn't going to let them down under any circumstances, not even for him. She could only leave if they found a reliable replacement.

Luke's face set in obstinate lines. 'You're being too conscientious. No one's indispensable.'

'I know, but they've already been let down once. Oh, darling'—she knelt beside him and put her arms round his neck—'I'm just as keen to get married as you are, but I must play fair. You do see that?'

She looked at him anxiously, and Luke's ill humour went as quickly as it had come. 'I suppose I can learn to be patient, though it means we'll only be able to see each other at weekends,' he said grudgingly.

Later they telephoned their news to Jill's family and to Luke's grandparents. Dr Bentley sounded surprised but pleased, and said that he and Marcia would come round to the hospital that evening, since Jill wasn't free to go out. The Haddons were quite obviously delighted, and the Professor was more talkative than usual.

He agreed with Jill that she must not leave her post until it had been adequately filled.

'Don't let Luke bully you, my dear. Stand up to him! Be firm!'

Mrs Haddon said that if Luke chose to marry a professional woman he had to consider her career as well as his own. Was there a hint of criticism in the gentle voice? Did Mrs Haddon disapprove of working women? Jill asked this uncertainly, and was relieved by her answer.

'Of course I don't disapprove! I'm sure you're clever enough to combine marriage and a career. Luke needs a girl who can meet him on equal terms. He would never be happy with just a pretty face.'

Luke was registering increasing impatience. He signalled to Jill to end the conversation, and when she shook her head snatched the receiver from her. He laughed at his grandmother's next remark, and told her that he was on the line now, not Jill.

'We'll ring again tomorrow, Grandma. Goodbye.' He turned and smiled at Jill. 'She hopes we won't leave it too long before we start a family. They'd be charmed to have some great-grandchildren!'

Plenty of women managed families and careers, Jill thought. She would take some time off when they first got married, then look around for a job near Queen's. Later on, when the children came, she would do part-time work, perhaps be a part-time anaesthetist.

'Why not?' Luke agreed. 'There are plenty of openings in anaesthetics.'

She stroked his dark hair lovingly. 'I'm the luckiest girl in the world. So many women have to choose between marriage and a career. It must be awful having to make a decision like that, though if I had to I know which I'd choose.'

Her smile made it plain what she meant by that remark, and Luke drew her closer and kissed her long and lovingly.

'We'll have such fun, sweetheart, when we're married. We'll be busy, both of us, and we may not have much time together at first'—when the telephone started to ring he held on to her for a few moments longer before picking the receiver up and putting his palm across the mouthpiece—'but the time we do have together will be doubly precious.'

Then he handed her the receiver and walked over to the window, while Jill listened to the Accident Officer telling her about a small boy with a broken arm, who needed an anaesthetic.